Betrayal

To June

Love

[signature]

xx

Barbara has recently relocated to North Yorkshire to be amongst the wonderful countryside where on her long walks she contemplates her new chapters, and stories for following work.

Never one to let time stand still, Barbara is always busy with new projects and now her future looks as though a visit to warmer climes in the Mediterranean is planned.

She is currently working on her third novel, *Denial*, which follows on from *Betrayal* and *A Rose Can Bloom in Autumn*.

Her passion for writing began at a young age whilst at school and it is now that her dreams are coming true with the success of her first novel; her work has attracted a great deal of interest with commissions from abroad.

Betrayal

Barbara Byford

Betrayal

Olympia Publishers
London

www.olympiapublishers.com
OLYMPIA PAPERBACK EDITION

A CIP catalogue record for this title is
available from the British Library.

ISBN: 978-1-84897-264-3

(Olympia Publishers is a part of Ashwell Publishing Ltd)

First Published in 2012

Olympia Publishers
60 Cannon Street
London
EC4N 6NP

Printed in Great Britain

Emotions are a wonderful natural gift – never be afraid to show them.

True friends never lose their faith in you...

Chapter 1

Liz walked back into the lounge area of their home stunned and amazed and looked at the other three women. She was so excited that at first she found it difficult to speak. Her eyes met Max's for help to get her words out. She was shaking with excitement.

"They want to publish don't they?" enthused Max, so excitedly for her partner as she took her hand and hugged her.

The other two women looked on in bewilderment not quite knowing what was happening.

"Come on," said Rose smiling at them "What's this all about? Share with us then," as she looked at them so happy together for once.

When the excitement had died down, Rose realised that this was the first time she had seen Liz and Max even touching each other in the past few weeks.

Liz in her own quiet way, yet so excitedly, began to relay the story of the diary that she had kept whilst on her road to recovery. The publishers had read the diary and now wanted her to turn it into a book and had asked her to complete this with a co-writer. They were talking of film, radio and theatre rights, radio and television interviews; it seemed Liz would soon be in huge demand.

Max almost immediately reverted to the woman that they all knew, excitable, proud, exasperating even, as she too joined in the now high spirited conversation. She was so full of pride and overjoyed for her partner. The champagne was opened and they all raised their glasses to their 'budding author'. The excitement was catching and soon they were all celebrating happily for Liz.

Max immediately for once took over and decided that the rest of the day would be taken off from work, painting and training, whatever they had planned as they began to relax. This was the first time in a while they had all been together in such a light mood. It was as if they had taken a step back in time and everything was back to how it had been before they had gone to America.

Liz quickly called her personal trainers – now very close friends Michael and Sarah, who straight away came to join in on their celebrations. They were as thrilled for her as everyone else and the rest of the afternoon was spent in very high spirits. There was much laughter and joy as they all talked about the forthcoming few months.

The following day's training programme was cancelled by Michael as too many bottles of champagne were opened. It turned into an impromptu party with laughter and happiness, something which had been severely lacking lately.

There was so much excitement and joy as they all talked about the forthcoming few months. Gradually as the afternoon turned into evening Rose somehow managed to put a meal of sorts together with plenty of French bread and cheeses as they all began to throw caution to the wind and relax, something they had not done for a while.

When their guests had gone Mary and Rose left to return to their home. Liz looked at Max and for the first time in ages really liked what she saw.

"Come on," she whispered, "let's go to bed."

Max looked at her, her eyes now full of love for her partner and took her hand as they climbed the stone stairs for the first time in ages – together. Once in the bedroom Max held Liz closely and began to kiss her passionately. Liz eagerly responded, thrilled that her partner was being so gentle and loving. She began to undress Max exploring her body with her hands and mouth. For hours they took each other on a journey that was a different pace from how things had been recently.

Max was gentle, reassuring and so attentive. Liz was in her element as she felt that at last her partner had returned to the woman she had fallen in love with nearly seven years ago. Max teased and tormented Liz with her hands and mouth until finally as her fingers entered her, Liz released cries of ecstasy again and again.

The passion was at its height for many hours as Liz responded to Max ensuring she was also totally satisfied. Max now enjoyed more vigorous lovemaking, demanding more and more from Liz who obliged her whilst also taking pleasure in her, giving her lover so much satisfaction. For hours they took each other on a journey that was a different pace from how things had been recently. Eventually exhausted, they both fell into a deep restful sleep as they once used to do.

The next morning Max looked at Liz as she slept soundly. Liz did not drink much these days and Max knew she would sleep for a while longer as they had all drunk more than usual. For once there was a more relaxed look on Liz's her face and not the worried concerned look that was usually on it. Max held her again and thought about their relationship. She had to make everything right between them and vowed to try and take things easier with Liz, take things at a slower pace – give more. As she continued to watch Liz her hand began to gently caress her. She began to kiss her shoulder gently and then Liz stirred. She looked deeply into Max's eyes as she spoke.

"Hi."

"Hi you," smiled Max as she held her tighter. Her hand began to wander over her body and as Liz responded to her touch, they again took each other to a point of no return.

There were no interruptions as they lay there dozing, talking and just enjoying each other, just the two of them. In hindsight Liz thought everything was back on track, that Max was back to her normal self, that they would salvage what had broken between them – but then hindsight could be sometimes be dangerous.

Eventually after showering and dressing they descended downstairs to find the lounge clear of all remains of the day before. All was tidy and a note had been left for them. Breakfast whenever you are ready at ours, the note read. Rose had been in and tidied and for once they were going to their home through the adjoining corridor between the two homes.

"This is how it should be Max," whispered Liz treasuring every moment since last night.

They walked next door and had a leisurely day with the others, no tension or pressure just relaxing. They were all tired from the day and night before, especially Liz and Max.

Later Liz even managed to entice Max out for a walk through the grounds talking about everything and nothing; it was as if nothing was wrong it had all been repaired.

They went home arm in arm and curled up on the large cushions in front of the fire that afternoon. The winter nights were drawing in and they spent the evening chatting and laughing finally going up to bed contently, making love again and again until they finally slept until the morning.

Back to normal were Liz's final thoughts as she fell asleep in her beloved partner's arms.

After a day or so the celebrations were over and Liz, Max, Mary and Rose contemplated the new era that they were now entering into. Once more their lives were about to change. The publication of Liz's book would ensure that their very private lives that Mary in particular, had relentlessly protected would now become scrutinised and more unrestricted.

Naturally they were all thrilled for Liz, as since their return from America six months ago her purpose in life had just seemed to be working out in the gym and spending time in the village at the business. She had seemed content with her life they all thought.

America had proved to be a huge escape for Liz in many ways. Upon their return the relationship between Max and Liz had been at its height and could not have been more perfect.

In America Liz relished the space and the freedom it had given her and she realised she wanted more of it now she was back in Scotland. Her relationship with Max was also beginning to change.

There was some apprehension from Mary; she knew their once private, incredibly extravagant and steady lives that she had unfailingly guarded would be changing yet again, but was it for the better? She was ruthless in her pursuit to ensure that Max her twin sister became the internationally famous artist and lived up to the reputation that she was moulding for her. She was working so very hard for her sister and she knew one day her dream would be fulfilled!

Up until the last year or so their lives had revolved around Liz while she recovered from the horrors of five years ago. However, she was as fully recovered as she ever would be. Perhaps now they all needed to follow their own destiny and whatever it held for them she wondered.

Mary thought about Max who had been the rock that Liz needed to help her recover. Now it was her sister's turn to be the famous one. Yes she was very close to Liz but her sister as always came first in her life. Nothing and no one would stop her in her dream for Max.

She had always ensured her twin came first in everything and it looked as if the spotlight would once again be on the wonderfully perfect Liz. There was a hint of jealousy creeping in, something both sisters could fall prey too.

The timing was all wrong for her plans. She was so concerned that they needed to concentrate on Max 100% and could not afford to get sidetracked with anything else. The publication of the book may prove to be this distraction if she did not take over the situation. She would have a quiet word with Rose to ensure that they fully focused on Max.

Max treasured Liz and was an amazing help in her recovery, continuously working with her helping her, encouraging and totally supporting her in all that she struggled to do. Liz had very rarely been allowed out of Max's sight until recently, since America. The last six months in fact had seen a gradual change in all of their relationships in very different ways.

Max had a temper which had been heavily controlled for years but, there were often hints of it surfacing to the top these days as her work demanded more and more of her time. This was evident especially when she was working on a commission or towards an exhibition – both of which were becoming more frequent thanks to the scheduling of Mary and Rose.

Peter their agent would arrange the venues and the two women would organise the finer details. Mary would encourage Peter to book as many exhibitions and interviews as possible for Max. She was conscious she was pushing her sister more and more and she knew that the relationship between Liz and Max was suffering. Max did not speak about it but Mary knew her twin so well.

She knew that the frenzied pace that Max now painted at would be hard to slow down from.

She deduced that Liz probably had problems with Max and more often than not when the four of them did get together she noticed how much quieter Liz was nowadays. The laughter and light atmosphere in the house was not so evident. Everything was so serious these days. Those times when they were all together were becoming less frequent now. Rose and Mary would spend their evenings planning the next exhibition or trip for Max. Liz would not always be there even for dinner now.

Mary never saw any evidence of Liz being hurt physically but she just felt things were not quite right between the couple. If Max was hurting her she didn't think Liz would ever get over it considering her past experience with Sam. She should make more time for Liz and vowed she would once the book was finished and the amount of exhibitions had reduced. Next year was going to be their busiest year ever with numerous events. She knew it must be difficult at times living with Max.

The person that could make her sister content and suppress her temper was a godsend at this particular time, but Liz would just have to take a back seat for a while. It also took the pressure off Mary if someone else was trying to tame Max as she became more and more headstrong in her life.

The past few years had been wonderful, dreadful, horrific, exciting, a multitude of experiences, but above all they had all stuck together and become very close to each other. Their lives were interwoven with each other. This was now to change.

Her relationship with Rose was becoming strained sometimes. She knew deep down she wasn't making the right time for Rose either. They had become almost complacent with each other and were certainly not the loving steady couple they once were. Her life now was her sister.

Rose seemed to be distracted by something at the moment and was certainly not the Rose she had first known and had fallen in love with. Life just seemed so different from when the four of them all started to share their home and much of their lives together. She thought perhaps it was the pressure that she was inadvertently putting Max under which was affecting them all.

She knew things were not quite right in their relationship and couldn't remember the last time they had been together physically yet it did not seem to bother either of them. Very often Rose would sleep in one of the spare rooms feigning headaches or over tiredness as she was often unable to sleep. Mary wasn't quite as concerned anymore. Her mind was focused on her sister.

Rose thought long and hard about what the future might bring. She and Mary did not have quite the same loving relationship they once had. Perhaps they took each other too much for granted? They were always there for each other, always supporting each other but maybe not quite as deeply in love as they once were. It was a different bond they had now. There was no spark between them, although as Rose thought there never was a spark. There would never be anyone like Liz. She would never feel the deep love she still had for Liz after all these years.

She was now helping Mary more than ever as they worked hard with Peter their agent to book exhibition after exhibition for Max in the quest for her supremacy in the art world. Liz, she knew was being left behind and she noticed how she was becoming more and more withdrawn out of the four of them.

Liz began to spend more time away from the home and more time in the village and the business with the people who worked for her. She enjoyed the company of the villagers and they loved having her around them. They also all began to notice just how much more time she was spending at the business and especially the stables.

Max and Mary had ensured Liz owned the business outright and had signed it all over to her after the 'accident'. She had grossed a fortune out of the business and as usual had invested very wisely indeed.

Liz was spending more and more of her time with Michael and Sarah in the gym as well. Rose was seeing less and less of the person she had tried to protect from the past.

She thought daily about the earlier period in her life and hoped so much that it was never going to rear its head. For all these years she had kept a brave face on things and she knew no one suspected anything. As time had gone on her relationship with Mary began to change. They were not the steady loving couple they once were. Sometimes she chose to sleep in another room when her brain was in overdrive.

She sometimes found it hard to unwind but the reason was different from that of Max. She had discovered some pills on the internet that would help her keep up at the frenzied pace that Mary was working at and she found she needed far less sleep nowadays.

She had lost some weight over the last few years through worry and she had recently begun to feel, through her own paranoia, that her world was on the verge of crumbling right in front of her.

She knew the book that Liz was going to co-write would be truthful and tasteful and be so helpful for other people who had suffered brain injuries. She worried however that the publication of it would also bring to the surface people from her past as they began to read it.

The hype surrounding the publication when it was completed would attract a lot of people and she began to feel more and more concerned. This was not how their lives should be. She thought to herself it was all beginning to change and not necessarily for the better.

Rose knew eventually there would be media frenzy due to the fact of who Liz and Max were. There was already talk about film rights so the publishers were obviously very confident that the book would be a success. No, her main concern was the people who were going to read it, the people from her past that was the worry.

Whatever anybody felt about Liz, she was one of the most truthful and honest people she had ever met in her life. Deep down she knew she was still in love with Liz and she knew, if given the encouragement, she would end her relationship with Mary at the drop of a hat to be with her. She had lived with that thought for as long as she had known Liz. Their lives had been reasonably private up until now, Mary had succeeded in shielding them all but now that would change. They lived in their own bubble extravagantly wanting for nothing.

Max was so happy for Liz, at long last she had an aim in life. Recently she had begun to hate herself knowing that she now had begun to mistreat Liz. When she was painting she knew her mood changed dramatically and sometimes she just could not slow down. She could not switch off, and more and more frequently would make huge demands on Liz physically and mentally.

On these occasions, in the morning when she looked at Liz, seeing the bite marks she hated herself. She wondered why Liz never asked her why she had done these things to her. Why had she treated her so disrespectfully? Liz never mentioned it. They needed to talk and talk soon.

Originally they had been playful little bites but now they were becoming more evident and hurtful, she hated herself but she couldn't stop herself in these situations. It was her way of unwinding and she knew she was too forceful and insensitive with Liz. Then she said to herself with her other voice in her head, it was not as if Liz complained. She would always give herself to Max totally – eventually. She never refused her really she thought.

She was always full of remorse the next day and begged Liz to forgive her when she had woken. She made every effort she could to make things right and then for a few days things were back to how they should be. Liz always forgave her she never complained. The pressure was on and growing for Max. Liz was however now questioning her actions, but silently.

Maybe the writing would help them both to sort their relationship out. Maybe Liz would feel the same passion that she felt when she was painting. Perhaps she too would find it hard to come down from the thrill of writing. It was a drug to her which sent her on an unbelievable high and which was so difficult to come down from.

Now however, Max was as excited as she possibly could be. Her partner was at last turning the corner of what had been a rather strange year. In the five years since the 'accident' as they called it, Liz had not really seemed to have had much of a purpose in life other than get fully fit and well. The business in the village was in a place where it ticked over very successfully financially. Liz was amassing a fortune.

Liz would spend several afternoons a week there but other than that Liz did nothing else. Now, suddenly she was in demand, her mobile which seemed to have been dormant for most of the time was now very quickly coming back to life. Max thought she would buy her a new top of the range model and she ordered one. Liz was always spoiling her with gifts perhaps she should follow suit more.

For Liz the knowledge that she was going to help turn her diaries into a book was a dream come true. She now had a structured purpose in life. She knew she would be able to escape from the pressure and turmoil that was manifesting itself in the household with the other three women. She could lose herself in her own bubble once more with the co-writer and escape the tension.

Her relationship which was once so perfect now was turning into one which reminded her of the dark times she had with Sam. She began to feel as though everything was all her fault as Max seemed to take everything for granted.

She had been used to being made to feel inferior for much of her younger life. She had grown up knowing violence, hatred, jealously and despair. It was just following her around again.

Liz had constantly made excuses to herself for Max's behaviour and had encouraged her with the other three on her painting for a long time. Liz travelled with Max supporting her and often paying for the two of them personally to stay in marvellously expensive hotels. Only the best for her Max and she thoroughly enjoyed spoiling her but now she was wondering if she really wanted all the travelling anymore.

Liz was tired and almost felt the need to settle, put down some roots but where? She was also beginning to find the winters in the Highlands too cold. Her body with all its battle scars and repaired broken bones were beginning to react to the severe cold as it ached more and more in the winters. She was beginning to think about living in warmer countries. America had been a wonderful experience but it had also unsettled her tremendously.

Max had helped her all these years in her recovery always attending the hospital appointments with her, ensuring she never exceeded anything. Max had always been there for her but now things were changing. She was beginning to question decisions being made for her now. She was beginning to ask a lot of questions about herself too.

Liz began to feel slightly left out of things but then as Max would cuttingly often remind her, she had her physical fitness campaign and her friends Michael and Sarah were always at her side. In these moments Max would throw a few more hurtful comments to her showing her jealousy and temper which up until now were usually kept under control.

Liz would often ask herself why they were not relying on Peter their agent for all of this planning as she saw how involved and engrossed they were. She noticed how happy they all were but she did not quite share the same enthusiasm anymore.

Maybe she would call her dearest friend Peter and have a gentle but concerned word, they had not spoken for a few days and she did not want to cause an upset or question things – until now. She knew how important the work was for Max, she just was not as involved as the other three.

Liz still loved Max and would have once gone to the ends of the world for her. Would she now? She wondered as she began to question herself more and more. She was also aware that she was beginning to enjoy her own space.

Max was beginning to hurt her mentally and physically. The excitement she felt when she was with Max was not as strong as it had been. The declarations of love were not as forthcoming now as they once were. Nothing was the same any more.

Liz knew she couldn't pretend it didn't hurt her anymore. She needed to talk to Max before things got out of hand. After all she had been down this road before with Sam. More and more she felt as though things were her fault as she tried so hard to accommodate Max. At first she would pretend to be asleep when Max eventually came to bed and was left alone.

As Max became under more pressure, she would paint into the early hours, drinking as she painted. Sometimes she would even paint all through the night. Now more often than not she would come to bed the worse for wear and make demands on Liz, waking her up and taking her immediately whilst climaxing herself.

The gentleness had gone now. When Max needed something she had to have it instantly. Yes the writing of the book was going to change their lives for ever each in a very different way.

Individually they began to take stock of their lives thinking about their history, past loves and life before they all met. They each wondered how much their futures were going to change now that their so very private lives were going to become more public.

For each of them the publication of the book spelt excitement, trepidation, relief, horror and dread.

Chapter two

≋

Liz

Liz's childhood had been nothing short of painful. She was born to parents who really didn't have the time or the money to care for her properly. She was one of six children and had constantly been reminded that she was a mistake for as long as she could remember. She regularly wished she had not been born and could sink into dark times of depression fairly easily.

Her school years were where she relished her life. She threw herself into sports and so as to prevent being at home this meant her training before and after school. The least amount of time she had to spend in the place called home the better.

Her parents drank, smoked and constantly argued so it was not the ideal life at all. Luckily she had the brains and the support of several teachers at school to try to overcome these times. She was very athletic and adored sports.

As she began to grow into adolescence her senses were awoken to other girls in the school. She was clever and also read a great deal always busy doing something.

She was popular in a quiet sort of way and everyone around her enjoyed being around her. Several boys asked her out on dates and she accepted them having an agreeable time until it was time to say goodnight. As far as boys went it was a kiss at the end of the evening and nothing else. Once or twice they began to try their luck and take things further but she always stopped them.

It was not what she wanted and she knew she was attracted to girls far more. She was not troubled by her sexuality and never questioned it; she was perfectly at ease with it.

The girls in the sixth form a grade higher than her were to her, superstars, she idolised them. They were young women and she enjoyed being with them. It became common knowledge around school that her home life was deplorable and her friends ensured that she spent as little time as possible there. When she was sixteen her parents demanded that she left school and get a job.

It would be a sad day when she left as she had wanted to get qualifications and make something of herself. She was determined to make something of her life and not live in the squalor that was supposedly her home. Her teacher pleaded with her parents to let her stay on to the sixth form getting her grades and eventually wore them down.

They had a sixth form block at her school solely for sixth formers and this was her solitude. She trained every night for whatever sport or team she was playing for.

Her last year there was perfect and she fell in love for the first time. A girl in the upper sixth had caught her eye; unknown to her this girl had been looking out for Liz and had become attracted to her. They struck up a friendship in the library and would often meet up there after school and study together.

Eventually the girl Anne invited her out. Liz was thrilled, her first date with another female. A gentle love affair began and they thought they would die if they split up.

Anne had awoken Liz's senses and feelings and for several months they enjoyed being with each other. Both young and exploring their inner feelings they professed undying love for one another and planned to run away together. They experimented with each other and

Liz knew that being with a woman was the right thing. Of course it didn't last. Anne left school and went to college leaving Liz bereft, almost inconsolable.

Eventually the time came for Liz to leave school and she dutifully got a job in an office hating it. After a couple of months she made a decision which would change her life for ever.

Her parents were demanding so much board off her she had very little spare money but again she spent as much time away from home as she could.

She was seventeen and at a crossroads in her life. She had started going to pubs with some girls from the office and realised that she could get a job in a pub. She loved meeting people and although she was not 18 she could at a pinch pass for that age. Anyway, she thought, I am 18 in a few months. She left the office job as soon as she could.

For the next four months she worked in a bar in London and thoroughly enjoyed it making friends easily. Her manager realised that she had a flair for the catering side as she waited at table and helped in the kitchen.

"What you need to do is get some qualifications, work in some kitchens and I think you could make something of yourself," he told her.

She thought about what he had said and realised that that was where her path lay. She worked hard and then after a year met up with some friends who were travelling around Europe. When she was asked to join them she jumped at the chance.

She had moved out from home over a year ago. She and her parents had had a terrible row, the worst one yet. They were relying on her to provide them with money but now she was standing up for herself.

Her life had been surrounded by rows, alcohol and violence and she wanted out. She hated confrontation and would often go along with things to keep the peace. In the heat of the final row in front of her three brothers and two sisters she was told things she never had been told before. She had caused the family to become penniless. She was and had been too expensive to keep.

They constantly told her they wished they had given her up for adoption. She didn't fit in and indeed her father thought perhaps she had been mixed up at birth. She didn't resemble anyone in the family. They had no feelings for her, she was an outcast. Her skin was slightly darker than anyone – her brothers and sisters were all fair skinned.

Her siblings all worked. None of them had got qualifications. They went straight to work and could not understand her need to explore and learn so much. She was a mouth that was too expensive to feed. She was odd, strange and didn't like boys, she was a freak. The final insult was when she was summoned to the lounge by her parents. Her brother had spotted her with another girl. Everything came out and her father was puce in the face looking as if he would burst.

He demanded she left and she was terrified that he would raise his hand to her again. She had known a life of violence. It was all she knew. It was time for her to leave forever.

She took one final look around the lounge.

"You will never see or hear from me again," she said quietly.

The hurtful things that had been said would stay with her for a while but in time she would forgive and forget. There was not a bad bone in her body, she was convinced deep down they loved her. She clung onto that dream for many years. Her adventure was about to begin. She took one last look around the room; her mother knew that when Liz said something she meant it.

Liz's eyes were wide with anger and yet, there was a look of love in them. Her father, tall, large and red faced, stared at her. She had no feelings either way for him. She just thought of him as the man who constantly hit her mother.

"Go now," he said with a quieter voice now. "Go now before I really hurt you."

He had slapped her so many times around the face; and her mother had used her as a punch bag in their drunken state when she had tried so hard to make them love her. All she wanted in her life was the love of two parents a love she never really knew.

It was time to go. She would never return and would keep to her word. She was determined to find true love and have a loving relationship. She wanted to find a soul mate unlike the relationship her parents had. She could only remember them shouting, drinking and being violent towards each other. Surely there had to be more to life than this. There must be people who found true love and happiness? That was all she wanted.

She was determined to make something of her life. All she could remember was being told she was nothing. She would never make anything of herself. She was a dreamer. She belonged in an office providing money for the rest of the family like her brothers and sisters.

Who did she think she was imagining she could be something other than a provider of food for the table?

Eventually she was pushed too far. When this happened she rebelled.

To travel abroad was her excuse, her way out and she excitedly packed a rucksack as she set off on her adventures with the other girls. Some were gay some were straight. No one was in a relationship with anyone and they intended to attend the festivals all over Europe.

They found work along the way and she was so happy working in hotels learning the trade. She made friends easily and had a couple of short term relationships but nothing serious. Her affairs had been exciting but not meaningful. She knew deep down what she was looking for in a woman. Her confidence grew and grew and although she was an exciting woman in her own right she could be slightly reticent yet so friendly. People enjoyed being around her and she was so effortlessly breathtaking.

They arrived in Italy and a strange feeling overcame her. She suddenly felt at home there and in the last few months of their gap year she realised that Italy was where she wanted to live. She adored the place and decided she was going to do some courses at a college there. She was 19.

The next year was spent studying in Geneva at a college. She made a lot of friends and was hugely popular. She learnt the language and had her first serious relationship. She learnt how to love a woman and finally accept love. For the first time in her life she felt better, confident about herself. With encouragement she was able to show affection for another person without being ridiculed. She knew she had a nice figure, was reasonably attractive and was determined to make the best of herself. In fact she was very attractive she just did not realise it.

She learnt the very basics in catering and in her spare time worked in various clubs, bars and hotels to pay for her education. She never once gave a thought to her family – she had left all of that behind. One thing she had learnt about herself was that if pushed too far she could switch all emotions off.

She managed to put all of her childhood memories behind her. She parked them in her brain never to be opened again. She had cousins aunts and uncles but never made any attempt to keep in touch with them. They were all dead to her.

She was popular at college and lived in a room rented by one of the college lecturers. She treasured her time there and met some people who in years to come would become her greatest friends. Loyalty was her greatest quality in a friendship which would prove to be so valuable in later years.

At the end of the term her lecturer suggested she went back to London and study at a well know Hotel College in Westminster.

"The qualification gained from there will take you through life and open doors for you. It is two years of your life that you will cherish for ever."

She listened carefully and realised he was giving her a chance to fulfil her dreams.

She loved Italy and did not want to leave but realised he was right. She vowed that one day she would return to live there. How true this was to become.

She travelled back to London and was successful in her interview for the college. It was during this time she almost immediately met Rose who would become one of her greatest and most loyal friends. Rose had been in love with Liz ever since she met her and apart from an early declaration of love and one kiss, had remained in Liz's life knowing she would never be more than a friend.

Then of course Liz met the love of her life, Sam. Several weeks into the first term at college Sam strode boldly into the lecture room and immediately they were smitten with each other. The rest was history.

The next twelve years were spent building their business into a hugely successful empire. As their careers rose in stature, their relationship towards the end suffered. Sam often dabbled in soft drugs and had a string of affairs with other women unknown to Liz.

Liz seemed oblivious to it all and merely continued to ensure that their business was ranked among the best in the country and it was. Despite the drugs and other women Sam worked as hard as Liz and together they became famous in London attaining celebrity status, constantly in the papers and being interviewed on TV and radio. Yes they had made a name for themselves in the world of corporate entertaining.

The end of the relationship came quickly and abruptly. Liz had walked in on Sam in bed with two other women. Hurt beyond belief, she had driven to her accountants and eight hours later, she had bought out Sam. She now owned the whole business.

She had decided in an instant the relationship was over, there was no room for excuses and apologies it was finished. Her home life had ensured that once she was hurt by anyone, the relationship or friendship was finished.

It was when she met Max, six months after splitting with Sam, that she felt her life was totally worth living again and she threw herself heart and soul into the relationship. Max had been real the love of her life she thought – until now. Now she doubted herself and her relationship with Max.

Out of the three women Liz was the only one not born into money. It was her sheer determination that had enabled her to become the wealthiest of all of them.

Chapter 3

Max

Max and Mary were both sent to boarding school at a very young age in Edinburgh. Money was no object and their parents wanted the best for their two girls. One day the girls would inherit the large estate so their education was paramount. Once the schooling had finished, it was Max who wanted to carry on at Art College. Her talent had a long time ago been recognised.

Mary would return home to gain knowledge of the family business. It was obvious to her parents that Max was going to be a successful artist. Whilst at boarding school she had a couple of relationships with other girls. Max had known from as early as she could remember about her sexuality unlike her sister.

The thought of being with another man repulsed her. She once or twice wondered if that had anything to do with one of the estate workers who had begun to abuse her when she was about four or five. Another worker realised what was happening after he heard her shouting and screaming in a barn and came to the rescue. Her eyes were wild with a fury that was frightening for someone so young. There was a terrible temper deep rooted in the young girl. She was then and always would be a loose cannon.

From a very early age she had courage, charisma and confidence the three c's as their mother called it. She was also tempestuous, fiery and volatile. There was a down side though to her makeup.

She could be full of enthusiasm and energy one day and completely the opposite the next. Almost bipolar she had mood swings which worried everyone. Her parents despaired of her sometimes, yet treasured her.

Her appearance had remained the same throughout the years. She had always worn her hair long. It was naturally curly and this made her look even more bohemian than ever. She had a terrible temper which she managed to keep under control – just – for years.

Her dress sense had never faltered. She always wore layers and layers of colourful cottons and during the years of many different fashions, it never faltered. She was a striking figure, tall and elegant and oozed personality. Whatever she was doing she threw herself into it whole heartedly. The couple of girlfriends at school had been almost platonic. She knew deep down she needed someone as explosive as herself and would one day find that person. Her father chose not to talk about that side of her life and this suited him. He adored both of his daughters.

Max had been recommended by the school to go to Art College. Here she blossomed and her talent, raw though it was, shone through. She made many friends and realised that her art would be her vocation. Max had a huge flat in the city near to the college and whenever Mary would stay she would spend a great deal of her time tidying it up.

Everything with Max was always in a mess yet she knew just where to find everything at a drop of a hat. She did all of the usual things that students do and even had a 'proper' but short relationship as she called it.

She would spend the holidays back at home and would often take some friends too for the break.

"I don't mind what you do," pleaded their mother, "just none of those herbal cigarettes you seem so fond of."

Mary would always find the usual list of rules and regulations funny as she watched Max being lectured to by their mother.

"No sex, or drink in your suite either." The girls had a wing each of the huge hunting lodge which was their home.

Those three years at college were the first time the twins had been apart. Mary hated it but it was such a release to Max, it felt like freedom.

She had a new lecturer in her third and final year who was French, and within days Max became transfixed by her. She had never experienced these feelings before. She was nearly 20 and Marianne, she presumed must be at least 15 years older, although her body belied the fact. Max had a fixation about bodies – their lines and curves. Eventually she would paint nudes and be extremely in demand in the years to come.

Marianne was beautiful, chic, typically French and Max was falling hopelessly in love with her. Marianne knew how Max felt and would often suggest she come to her apartment to put in some extra hours learning about the history of various French artists. Marianne would toy with Max and sometimes tease her but she soon knew that she was beginning to feel the same way about her. More and more Max would go to make a move but Marianne would break away leaving Max forlorn.

"We cannot, I will lose my job," she would say although she wanted her so much.

Towards the end of the course, decisions had to be made. Marianne had been offered the job of a lifetime back home in Paris.

She knew Max had a talent so rare and she knew she could have both if she was clever. Max was awarded a scholarship miraculously, at the end of the term and was beside herself with grief knowing that Marianne would be going to Paris.

"Come with me then. You could paint and study for your scholarship in Paris, while I work at the university. We can be a couple there without any problems it will be easier," Marianne said as she looked into Max's eyes.

Max didn't need to be asked twice. She and Marianne went back home where Marianne would speak to father. The way she spoke to him was beautiful and father and mother were thrilled for Max. Mary was understandably upset at the thought of her twin moving to another country but she was so involved in the estate business. Their lives were changing.

"You can always fly over. It is not too long a flight," Max remarked excitedly.

Marianne explained that Max would be staying with her. She had an apartment which was large enough for the two of them. They set off as Max travelled with an allowance that had been agreed by her parents.

"Just think that when you are a well-known artist in the world – remember your old dad." their father chuckled her as he hugged her goodbye.

They set off for their adventure excited and with some trepidation. Marianne realised she had fallen in love with Max and as soon as they arrived at her apartment the moment they had both been waiting for happened.

It was Marianne who showed Max how to make a woman feel love and passion for the first time in her life. They unpacked the car and as soon as everything was in the apartment Marianne took Max and held her close to her kissing her passionately. She immediately and expertly undressed Max as they made their way to the bedroom. Here Marianne gently explored Max's body taking her to feelings she had never experienced before. Max thought she would explode as her body pulsated at every touch of the woman she had fallen in love with.

Marianne was in fact nearly twenty years older than Max and her experience in life and love was something that Max relished. They treasured each other and it was during the next couple of years that they settled into a very loving tactile relationship.

They spent their summers in the south of France it was perfect. Max painted during the day while Marianne lectured or taught privately. Max missed her parents and her sister more than she realised and they would ring regularly. Mary visited every 8 weeks.

Mary realised as soon as she was in the apartment that Max and Marianne were a couple and was slightly jealous to begin with. Someone had taken her baby sister from her. But it was clear that Max was in her element living in Paris, painting and in love. She was sure of herself and her eyes were ablaze with passion so strong, it was almost frightening.

As often the case things were too good to be true. It was not always enough for Marianne to go to work then come home. Max would always have a meal waiting with plenty of wine and would panic if she was late. Max attended the university but Marianne was determined their private lives would remain private.

Max never questioned anything. She was too infatuated. Mary on the other hand began to see through Marianne and started to plant seeds of doubt in Max's mind. Gradually Marianne spent less and less time at home often staying at the university due to late lectures or meetings. She was beginning to feel stifled by the mood swings of Max. She never knew what mood she would be in and she felt she needed her own space more and more.

Max was heartbroken and would spend hours talking to her twin about it all. She couldn't even remember the last time they had made love. Being with Marianne had proved to be the making of her though.

She was still volatile, tempestuous, and often childish but she felt there was a purpose to while she was with Marianne.

Marianne came home late one night to find Max fully clothed sobbing uncontrollably, sitting in the shower with the water running over her. She then realised how much their relationship had deteriorated and that it was mainly down to her. She had not supported Max enough in what she thought was a mental problem with her mood swings.

She should have got Max some professional help instead of staying away from her in the evenings. She was visibly upset and Marianne wished she had not kept the exhibition a surprise that was now taking place. She had wanted his moment for Max for such a long time and she now felt she had ruined it. Max had produced some wonderful work which was now being exhibited.

The reaction had been very positive but Marianne had focused too much on the work of Max and not on them as a couple. She knew that Max needed a lot of attention and she had failed her. The exhibition should have been a lovely surprise but instead she had driven Max to this awful state. She got into the shower with Max and cradled her like a child. She knew things were coming to an end. She tried to coax her to bed but it was too late for that. Max had made her mind up.

It was over. They talked late into the night. What had hurt Max the most was that her work was exhibited and yet she knew nothing about it?

After all, she wasn't allowed near the university it might compromise Marianne, she now thought bitterly.

The talking began to get spiteful and hurtful. Max had given everything to Marianne who in turn had taught her so much but it was finished. She would finish the scholarship. There was one more piece to complete then she would go home to Scotland. Now more than ever, she missed her family.

It was almost a relief for the pair of them when Max handed in the work. She began to pack the car that her father had paid for. It would take a couple of days to get home by driving and she would leave at the end of the week. She and Marianne although both hurt were going to have a meal out and be very mature about everything.

They had both adored each other and although it was over, they wanted it to be amicable. The chances of them meeting again were quite high as Marianne knew one day Max would be famous. The evening was wonderful and they realised they had done the right thing. There was no pressure on them now. Marianne had taught Max about life and how to live it, something that Max would never forget.

"You never forget you first love," Marianne had said gently.

They returned to the apartment for the last time. Marianne went to get some brandy for them. Tonight it felt right that they would be together again one last time. As she went to kitchen she answered the ringing phone.

She noticed they had missed several calls. Marianne was very quiet on the phone and instinctively Max knew something was very wrong. She came into the lounge ashen.

"It's Mary. There has been an accident."

Max rushed to the phone and spoke to Mary. Their parents had been driving home from Inverness. There had been an accident involving their car and a lorry. Her father had died, her mother was critically ill in hospital. Marianne was already packing for Max. Once off the phone she held Max for ages.

"We must be practical. You need to get home," she said gently.

Max was in a state of shock as Marianne took over. One of her good friends from the university would take the car to the ferry. Once in England one of the staff from the estate would fly down to pick it up and drive it back to Scotland. There was too much of Max's personal and professional items to trust on a train. Max was packed and the flight was booked for two hours' time. Marianne appeared with her bag packed.

"You don't think you're going on your own do you?"

She took her hand as they left together. Even now with their relationship over she was looking after Max.

They arrived at the hospital in time – just. Mary was there and they sat with their mother before she too died. The devastation was insurmountable. Marianne took care of the twins and was a true rock for the couple. The staff from the huge estate were marvellous support for them, everyone loved the girls especially Max, and who was becoming something of a star. After all, she had been living in Paris!

The funeral was attended by hundreds of mourners and it was about a month later when Marianne decided it was time to leave knowing that the business was now safe.

Mary was in a way quite pleased, as she could have Max to herself. She watched Max and Marianne say goodbye and wondered when they would ever see her again. Mary had looked on Marianne very differently while she had been staying with them. She knew they had shared a bed; she had heard them and could not understand the complex relationship they had.

Max came back into the house poured a large scotch and lit another French cigarette. She was hurting so much inside from everything and Mary knew it would be down to her to help and support Max. Max was where she belonged and Mary was there to look after everything – that was her duty, her goal in life.

Max and Marianne would talk a lot on the phone and then gradually over the months the calls stopped being quite so regular. Max was moving on and realised she had a responsibility to her sister and the estate they had inherited. As usual she threw herself into everything and still found time to paint. They both missed their parents terribly but, together they would overcome the grief. They were wealthy, beyond their wildest dreams.

Once or twice Max's head was turned by other women. She would travel into Inverness sometimes and meet up with some friends. For a while she burnt her bridges with too much drink and one night stands – she had several relationships but nothing too serious. Nothing was like the relationship she had had with Marianne She knew there was someone out there for her.

Over the next few years Max continued to paint and after a small exhibition in Inverness she was asked to travel to York as part of an exhibition with some other new artists. She was 38 and had already lived a life full of excitement, grief and heartbreak.

Mary was everything to Max now. She looked after the estate and Max. Mary was her accountant, agent, best friend – everything. Mary had found her niche with her sister. She was completely the opposite: calm, cool, always steadfast, a general plodder but wanted only the best for her sister.

Mary had worked hard over the years to promote Max and it was paying off. She had made Max what she was. They met up with the agent. His name was Peter and he had six artists he was looking after. They were introduced to Rose who would be looking after the food and fine wines. Rose had also organised the hotel and later arranged an apartment for them to stay and Mary took to her straight away.

The exhibition was in two days' time and Peter was going to hold a supper party for all of the artists at his home the evening before. He had arranged everything and it was then that Max and Mary really began to realise that their lives were changing. Peter and Rose both wanted their dear friend Liz to meet Max for the first time at his party. Peter was a marvellous matchmaker and these two belonged to each other, he was so sure.

Mary looked at Max as she came out of her bedroom. She looked wonderful, beautiful just gorgeous. Although they were identical it was Max who knew how to dress, – how to hold herself.

"That all comes from living in Paris," she laughed.

Mary always had dead straight hair that she kept tied back. Max was in another league and Mary idolised her.

"Enjoy your evening," Mary had said.

She too had a date and wanted to try to make the best of herself.

Arriving at Peter's home, Max was immediately whisked round the room and introduced to various people. It was apparent that these people had heard about Max's work and they talked excitedly about it all. Max had been there about an hour when it became obvious to her that someone quite well known had arrived. Various people left the room Max was in to make their way into yet another area. The house went on forever. She chatted intensely to a couple of critics when Peter came and steered her away.

"There is someone I want you to meet," he whispered as he ushered her out.

He led her through to yet another room where there was a break in the crowd almost immediately.

She saw Liz instantly as she talked and laughed with a small group of reporters. As if someone up above was watching over them she turned round. Max's heart missed a beat.

Max looked at Liz and was immediately smitten. She was beautiful, shorter than her, quite thin, expensively but casually dressed and her eyes spoke volumes to her. Liz had been hurt Max could tell, but her whole being told her she was one of the kindest people she had ever met.

"Hello I'm Liz." Liz held her hand out looking directly into Max's forlorn eyes.

Max took her hand. "Hello I'm Max."

By the end of the evening Max had fallen in love with Liz.

Chapter 4

Mary

Mary was always in the background of her twin sister Max and had been for as long as she could remember. She was everything Max was not. She was a thinker a planner she was calm, cool and never ever did anything on the spur of the moment. Everything had to be planned to the nth degree.

Although identical they were very different personalities. She idolised her parents they both did, but she idolised Max beyond belief. Max was always the star of the family she was raw and headstrong you never knew what Max was thinking or in fact was going to do next. You knew where you were with Mary. Strong reliable and steadfast their mother had said. She was just as beautiful as Max but in a different way.

She never really made the best of her features. She had the same piercing blue eyes but there was no fire in them they were never alight with the passion that Max possessed. She continually straightened her naturally curly hair.

She always looked old before her time. As soon as school was finished she immediately went to work with her father.

She knew at an early age that one day the two of them would inherit it all, she needed to know how to run it. She had a passion for work and poured everything into it but just went about things much quieter than Max. For many years she struggled with her sexuality not knowing who or what she really was. She and Max when they were at boarding school would talk about it. How she envied her sister – she knew from such an early age what she was and what she wanted but Mary just was confused.

Sex didn't seem to worry her, she had had no experiences and it was only when she left school she began to think about it more. Her dearly loved father introduced several eligible young men which she though very 'Bronte'. One took her interest slightly and they began to see each other. She would ring her sister at the art college and give her progress reports.

She missed her so much. Here she was in the Highlands talking to her sister about something she didn't really understand, eventually the relationship ended. She had not enjoyed the physical side, Max would listen intently and would add that maybe she had just not met the right one.

Mary still pushed herself to be successful in the business and she almost felt obliged to date the men that her father suggested. She so wanted his love.

After almost three years of seeing these men she decided enough was enough. She went to stay with Max before she went to Paris. Maybe I am not supposed to be with a man maybe I should be like you and be with women."

Max laughed

"You don't just decide to be gay, it is what is inside you that makes that decision."

They talked for ages about how she wanted father's approval and Max realised what a struggle she was having with her life.

"Let yourself go Mary. Do what your heart wants not your head you do not need approval for anything you do in life as long as it does not hurt anyone."

There, a simple yet so effective piece of advice from her wild sister.

Mary then went home. One of the girls on the estate had struck up a friendship with her a few weeks ago. She was slightly older than Mary but was always around. One day whilst chatting as usual Mary asked her if she fancied meeting for a drink.

Their parents didn't really approve of her 'mixing' with the estate people but this was a true act of defiance from Mary. She rang Max and told her she was so excited about meeting Patti and how reckless she felt.

Max gave her some advice

"Just be yourself don't expect too much if anything happens then just let it."

The evening was a success and Mary spent the night with Patti.

This was the first time she had been with a woman. Mary and Patti had spent the evening talking about her disastrous encounters with the men her father had chosen, Patti knew the score and how things were. It was common knowledge on the estate about Max and her sexuality but Mary was a mystery.

Patti suggested a night cap back at her flat. As she poured the malt whisky she looked at Mary straight in the eyes. As they drank their drinks they looked at each other, the tension mounting between them. Patti knew it was Mary's first time with another woman and she was so gentle with Mary never condescending just very loving.

She gently took her to a place she had never been before and it was then that Mary knew then where her path lay. They saw each other discreetly for nearly two years. Max was thrilled that her sister had finally found herself.

Mary was devastated when out of the blue Patti said she was leaving. She couldn't cope with being the discreet love interest. She couldn't compete with her father.

He had put two and two together and demanded she leave. Mary unleashed a torrent of abuse at her father and didn't think she would ever forgive him.

"You have to realise you will inherit this all one day I need you to bear me some grandchildren who will carry on the family name. Your sexuality could be the ruin of it all."

She screamed at him and ran after Patti.

"Let me come with you we can be together I don't care about all of this."

Patti looked at her from her car window

"But you do Mary you so do." And she was gone from her life for ever.

Mary was heartbroken and rang her sister who was in lectures. She drove to the college and waited for her. Max knew immediately something was wrong. They went back to the flat and drank copious amounts of red wine and Max smoked nonstop.

She was furious with their father but at least had the commonsense not to ring after drinking too much. They fell asleep in the lounge and needless to say the hangovers the next day were abominable. It was Max now who would look after her elder sister. She missed some lectures the next day which was unheard of especially with the scholarship she was working for.

They spent the day caring for each other and eventually in the afternoon they began to rally round.

There was a loud rap on the door and then it opened. It was Max's lecturer Marianne. She was very concerned for Max as she was her prodigy. She came into the lounge and saw Mary. Max explained to her what had happened. Mary thought she had explained too much and then realised that Marianne had a key. She put two and two together. Marianne stayed a while as they drank some wine

"Hair of the dog," said Max.

She drank quite heavily Mary thought now. After Marianne left Mary asked her sister what the situation was.

"Nothing to report there she replied – not yet anyway but I tell you I think she is the most amazing woman I have ever met."

She was her lecturer and was looking after her for the scholarship if she got it she would be going to Paris to paint. Mary was so upset. It looked as though she was losing her sister she would be even further away. Jealousy began to emerge.

It was an emotion she tried to keep at bay but it nagged away at her. Mary had a big problem with jealousy it was her Achilles heel – Max on the other hand had a temper that once unleashed could hurt people she loved the most – for years she was able to keep it at bay.

Of course Max got the scholarship and moved to Paris. She knew by now that they were a couple and began to plan for the future. She could see through Marianne and she knew Max would eventually come home with her tail between her legs. Her work was becoming recognised in the art world. Max was her project for the future.

She worked hard for her father they had put their differences aside thanks to mother. She feared Max would head off somewhere else in the world which left Mary with the burden on her shoulders. Mary knew what she wanted by now and would very often meet up with a woman, Karen, she had met at an art exhibition.

She loved art like her sister but she just enjoyed viewing she could not paint. They enjoyed a gentle relationship with each other for a long time. It just suited them both. There was no pressure on either of them. Karen would stay over a couple of times a month with Mary in her wing of the house.

Karen was by no means the love of her life but they enjoyed each other and there was no malice. They were both career minded and were striving for different things.

Karen proved to be very useful for Mary as she knew a lot people in the art world. She had heard of Max's work even now and helped Mary to plan for the future. It was such a gentle relationship that from the beginning Mary had no qualms about inviting her to meet her parents. Neither of them suspected they were having a relationship.

Her father was excited that interest was being taken in Max and all three of them began to put plans into motion to promote her work in the future. Karen began to stay at the estate more and more. Their father suggested she move in she could work from there and she had such good connections.

She moved into Mary's wing full-time. There was plenty of room there it also meant she and Mary could be together. Of course their mother knew what was going on, however they were discreet and as long as her father did not suspect anything she was happy about it, she certainly did not want another scene between Mary and her father. Whether or he not suspected they never knew he just never visited her side of the house. Karen was good for his daughter's future.

Mary of course shared her news and thoughts with her sister.

"I haven't even finished my scholarship," yet she cried. "Here you are planning my future."

"Yes but when you do I can help you, Karen has helped so much. You will be a huge star."

Max was so down and eventually told her sister about Marianne and how things were not so good. She felt as though her heart would break if it carried on like it was.

"You will work it out you always do."

They rang off Mary looked at Karen and realised how lucky she was. They may not be the most tactile of people but there was a mutual feeling of trust and admiration for each other. Now and again they would spend the night together and Karen knew she would be with Mary that night. Their lovemaking was for the first time in a long time fast, urgent and fulfilling.

Their relationship was turning a corner and Mary needed her desperately. They spent their days working hard, both sisters had never been shirkers. Everything was going well for the estate and Max. Their father had taken to Karen. She was an excellent businesswoman and they would spend time on estate business.

Mary sometimes was jealous of her but she realised she could bring even more business to the estate and her father liked her. Max had said she would be home next month and would more than likely be staying for good this time.

Mary thought she would burst with excitement her two favourite people other than her parents would all be together under the same roof.

The call came from the family friend Neil. He had driven to the lodge to deliver the devastating news about their parent's accident. Mary went into shock immediately and Karen took over. Mary had tried all afternoon to get through to Max. Once at the hospital knowing her father had died she waited and waited for news about her mother.

She was still in surgery. Eventually she managed to get through on the phone and spoke to Marianne. It was late and they had been out for a meal. Karen held her as she told her sister what had happened. That night was the longest night as she prayed Max would get back in time. She could charter a plane she thought but Marianne had managed to get flights organised. Max would be there by the morning.

She and Marianne arrived before nine the next day. Max looked ghostly white, in shock with Marianne by her side. She held onto her sister tightly the bond between them complete again. Three hours later their mother passed away.

She had never regained consciousness from the surgery and suffered a massive stroke. The twins sat in silence devastated. Marianne and Karen looked at them they would need so much support and help.

Differences would be put aside for this time in their lives. Karen organised everything the funeral etc. She helped to run things on the estate as the twins came to terms with their grief. Despite Max and Marianne's decision to end their relationship they began to rekindle it again even though they knew it would not last. Emotions were released in their lovemaking.

Mary began to emerge from her grief. Some of the people on the estate had spoken to her about Karen. Apparently she had been explaining to some of them about some plans she had which would probably mean some people would have to be laid off. One of the ladies who Mary was quite friendly with spoke to her confidentially about her fears.

Once or twice they had met up for a drink and a chat – Mary had always liked her and her family. They had a tied cottage on the estate and Karen was talking of using them for holiday homes.

Her back bristled. She went to speak to Max. She went straight into her side of the house and interrupted her and Marianne in the middle of a highly charged lovemaking session.

"I'm so sorry but this is urgent," she breathlessly announced.

Max and Marianne were furious with her as she begged forgiveness and pleaded with them to listen. Max made the mistake of choosing her sister over Marianne which in turn sealed the fate on their relationship. There was an unbreakable bond between the two sisters. They listened intently to what Mary had to say.

"How dare she? Who does she think she is?" Max was livid.

Marianne took charge of the situation. She suggested they do some investigating. Just how involved was Karen in the business. Why was she so involved? Her years of experience in life told her something was not right. She took it upon herself to dig deeper. Eventually a few weeks later she got the twins together. Karen was on a long phone call to her parents so was not around.

"Let's go for a walk where we can't be overheard." She didn't know how to bring the subject up. Max almost guessed and said.

"Just tell us straight. It's Karen and Dad isn't it?"

It appeared Karen and their father had started an affair several months before the accident. Max looked at Mary and held her as the colour drained from her face. No damage yet had been done to the business but they needed to act fast if they wanted to maintain the control he had left them.

Karen was a clever business woman who could ruin them. Mary was understandably devastated at being cheated on but more so knowing it had been with her father. A steeliness would now grow inside her over the years. She would never let anyone hurt her again and break her heart.

Max looked at Marianne with a longing look. Within hours Karen was escorted off the estate. Mary was again devastated. The last few months had been too much to bear. It seemed everything and everyone she loved had let her down. Still she had Max she knew she would never let her down.

Marianne stayed long enough to ensure the twins were once again in control of everything and their emotions she had been marvellous for them and they would never forget her wisdom. Max knew it was now over between them but agreed it was for the best. Mary's heart went out to her sister as she said her goodbyes. They looked at their father differently now.

As Max poured herself a drink and lit a cigarette she realised for the first time in her life that it was just her and Mary. Mary would look after her, care for her and above all make sure she made a success in the art world. She would protect her ruthlessly.

The twins were now 38 and it was just over two years since their parents had died. Max's work was becoming well known locally and one day Mary had a call from an agent/publicist called Peter who worked in York. She had read about him in some reviews. He was interested in new artists and wanted to exhibit some of their work

They agreed to meet up and she travelled down to Newcastle where he was working at that time. He asked a lot of questions about Max and her. She liked him feeling she could trust him. They signed a deal and then he introduced his friend called Rose.

She would be arranging accommodation, catering, refreshments anything they needed. Rose and Peter had known each other for years and she was a high-flyer in a company that he dealt with. She too wanted to know a bit more about the two of them. Mary and Max always were amazed at how interested people were in twins.

Despite all of the questions Mary found herself drawn to Rose. She was just what she admired in a woman. She was cool, calm and collected a planner. They were very similar and the feeling was mutual. Before the exhibition had begun they had started to see each other secretly. Mary had found what she was looking for at long last. They spoke on the phone regularly but agreed to keep their relationship quiet.

Max was the person they had to concentrate on. She was excited yet nervous about the evening and the exhibition this could be her big break. On the night of the party at Peter's, Mary and Rose saw each other and for the first time sealed their new relationship physically. It was not the most exciting sex that either of them had ever had but it was reassuring for them both. There was a feeling of contentment between them and a bond of friendship that would be tested throughout the years to come.

They realised that they were entering something that would last for many many years to come. Mary felt safe with Rose. She loved her as though she had never loved anyone else in her life before her.

Chapter 5

Rose

Rose was a born planner, old before her time. She was attractive but not overly so. She had before knowing Liz had a few girlfriends but nothing serious. As soon as she met Liz her heart was taken. She knew she could never compete with Sam and was bereft when they became an item.

There had been a terrible row between her and Sam after an evening when Liz came home battered and bruised. The bad feeling continued for the all the years they were together. She just dutifully played her part in the business organising planning and keeping her eye on Liz. Sam knew Rose was in love with Liz and would lay her life on the line for her.

Sam developed a very nasty streak in her and after being spoken to and treated like a child by Rose; she was encouraged by a small group of people who wanted revenge. She knew Rose had made a pass at Liz; Liz never had any secrets and after a few drinks had mistakenly told Sam. That was all the ammunition she needed to hurt Rose beyond belief and have her eating out of her hand. She was good at playing people and mind games and this would have her under her control once and for all.

Sam had often dabbled in soft drugs over the years but nothing too heavy but now after almost twelve years she was using them regularly and knew how to get hold of them. This was the sinister side of Sam which would inevitably be her undoing – Liz was oblivious to it all.

Sam very rarely was at the office, maybe once or twice a week, her time was spent on the road promoting the business and bringing in more and more orders. She turned up one day and spoke to Rose.

"I'd like you to come to dinner tonight. There are things that need to be said."

Rose agreed but was dreading it as no doubt there would be a scene. Sam knew how much Rose wanted Liz – she would see to it that she would have her and regret it. She then went on to chat to Liz and Rose watched her as she seemed to be so gentle and tender with her. Liz completely adored her and would have done anything for her.

Liz looked excited about the evening as if all the differences would be put aside. Sam left to prepare the evening. She was exceptionally house-proud almost to the point of a disorder and Liz knew she would ensure their apartment would be spotless as usual.

Later that evening Rose arrived. She had made a huge effort to look more up to date and not so dowdy and was wearing her hair down. It was a transformation.

Sam had prepared a wonderful meal and ensured that the drinks were flowing freely. The evening began with huge apologies from her about her behaviour towards Rose and after a while even Rose was taken in. Sam had done what she had to do with the drinks and waited for them to take effect.

After half an hour Liz began to appear different, giggly, carefree a completely different woman. Rose now began to feel different too and certainly her confidence was matching Sam's.

Sam then began to work on the pair of them she began to encourage Rose to tell Liz how she felt

"Go on tell her – tell her how much you want her, how much you love her," Sam whispered to Rose.

Rose then professed her undying love to Liz and instead of Liz rejecting her again she allowed Rose to kiss her as Sam encouraged the pair of them.

"Make love to her. Rose love her like this," as she began to caress Liz and kiss her.

She showed Rose how to make love to Liz. Sam led them to the bedroom as the two women began to make hard, fast, rough and violent love. Sam cajoled and egged Rose on; they didn't even realise that by now she had also undressed and joined them in a drug fuelled violent frenzy for the next few hours. Liz would never remember any of it she was too drugged.

It was several hours of shear heaven for Rose. Then Sam began to slap and punch Liz many times telling Rose that was how she liked it encouraging her to do the same to Liz.

By now Liz was barely conscious – so heavily drugged, but Rose and Sam had gone past the point of no return due to the drugs they were on as they continued to violate Liz. At last Rose had the woman of her dreams. It was wild frantic drug fuelled sex as the three of them enjoyed each other. Liz eventually fell into a deep sleep which would last for about 8 hours.

Sam now had Rose to herself and carried on. Rose didn't care what happened to her as Sam violently and aggressively had her too. She demanded the same from Rose and she obliged.

Rose awoke the next day and ached from head to toe as she slowly remembered explicitly what had happened during the night.

Sam walked into the room looking bright eyed. She had been up for hours, tidied up the apartment and was waiting for her crowning glory.

"So you're awake then." She smiled

"What happened Sam what's going on?" Rose was now scared.

"What happened Rose is you spent the evening with Liz and I. Look what you have done to her."

She pulled back the crumpled sheet to show the marks on Liz. The bites – the bruising were now beginning to show.

"Don't concern yourself Rose, Liz will not remember anything. She didn't last time. She'll think we had too much to drink – you on the other hand will remember everything."

Rose couldn't believe it and realised they had been drugged by Sam.

"You see Rose you have betrayed your dearest friend twice. Once by taking advantage of her situation and then twice by cheating on her with me."

The sly smile came over her. "And of course it's all on film let me show you."

Rose watched in horror as she began to play the cd. Rose's whole world came crashing down.

"You see Rose you will never get rid of me I will always have Liz for myself."

"But you prostituted Liz how could you do such a thing?" cried Rose

"Easy you are both so easy to play. Tell her what has happened and you will break her heart forever."

Rose knew there was no way out for her.

"You have been a challenge for me but I knew in the end I would win. Actually you were quite good in bed once I told you what I wanted."

That was it and Rose went to hit her. She was scared of her own anger.

"Oh no Rose, you will never get in my way again now go home, get to work and wait for my call."

Several days later Sam called on Rose. She needed her signature witnessed and Liz had suggested Rose do the signing. Sam would be on the road the next day so rode over on her powerful motorbike to her flat packed with documents she needed for the next day. She even thought she would spend the night there with Rose. She was dressed in her leathers and looked fantastic.

Always aware of being house proud she was the perfect guest and she took her boots off and was very polite to Rose. Rose had been a bag of nerves since that other evening and was drinking scotch. Sam drank scotch as a rule and Rose went to get a clean glass.

"Do you want ice?" She looked like a frightened rabbit, she was terrified of Sam and what had happened. She had not been to work telling Liz a lie that she was ill.

"Oh please."

Again Sam attended to Rose's glass and waited. Rose witnessed the signature it was a contract worth a great deal of money and Sam was extremely proud as she had won the contract on her own. She felt pleased with herself and needed some titillation. Rose was to be her stooge.

Within half an hour Rose's eyes were wild and Sam began to work her into frenzy.

She was proving to be very useful to her needs and she decided that this arrangement may need to be pursued on a longer and more regular basis. She had a couple of suppliers who had introduced her to these recreation drugs and soon she was using them regularly on Liz and whatever or whoever else took her fancy.

She was becoming hooked on them and the two suppliers ensured she was always fully stocked. Without Sam realising herself she was becoming dependent on these drugs which was the plan. She was playing into the hands of the two women who would eventually be responsible for so much more carnage.

Afterwards as the drug wore off Rose was again desolate.

"Remember Rose one day you will get the film so for now you need to indulge me." She grinned.

Rose realised she was now in so much trouble and had played into Sam's hands perfectly. Her nightmare had only just begun.

Luckily for Rose, anyway, a couple of months later on Christmas Eve Liz walked in on Sam and two other women. Liz never remembered that one of them was Emma the other someone called Christine. It was she who had supplied the drugs to Sam.

Sam had been to Rose's flat about half a dozen times afterwards and the same thing happened each time. Rose breathed a sense of relief as she looked after and cared for Liz during the next six months.

She hated herself but saying anything to her best friend now would in her mind be a terrible mistake. Liz was in terrible state and sinking into a form of depression, her heart broken already, this would make things worse. Rose always worried when Liz began to become depressed as it could take quite a long time to bring her out of it.

For years Rose worried about the CD but nothing ever came of it and it gradually became a blur. That night had been the most magical night of her life but Liz never knew anything about it. She began to rid herself of the memories especially the one with Sam. The relationship with Liz had finished horribly and Liz was now with Max.

She was with Mary life was good. Her relationship with Mary was in need of some help and she was sure they could rekindle the deep steady love they had. Deep down she was worrying herself and now was taking some pills she had found on the internet. She seemed to be so busy these days with Mary as they worked on Max's career and these pills just gave her the buzz she needed to keep up the pace they were working at.

She didn't feel there was anything wrong in taking the pills and even when she had a drink they didn't seem to affect her. It also meant she could complete so much more work.

The only problem she had was sleeping, and often she would sleep in a spare room. The physical side of their relationship needed some attention but then she thought neither or of them seemed too bothered about the lack of contact in that respect.

They had returned from America and Liz's book was going to be a great success she just knew it. Yet deep down she worried about what might happen once the book was published. There were certain people from the past who might resurface and for Liz to find out the terrible truth would be intolerable. It was five years since the accident and almost 7 years since that night when her nightmare had begun.

Chapter 6

Soon after the celebrations had died down several days later Max decided to buy Liz a new mobile phone, a top of the range all singing all dancing model she thought. Then she wondered if Liz would be able to operate a new gadget. Max and the others didn't really appreciate just how much progress Liz had made over the past few years. Maybe they didn't think she could improve anymore.

It was almost as if they didn't realise that actually Liz was probably the most alert of all of them, the most focused and certainly the most alcohol and drug free.

Liz had begun to notice the amount of alcohol that was being delivered into the house on a monthly basis. There was wine with every meal, drinks in the afternoon and then later on in the evening.

There was more and more entertaining with Mary and Rose ensuring that Max attracted as much publicity as possible in the big build up to her supremacy in the art world. There was more often than not guests staying next door with the three of them working so hard with interviews and photo shoots. Liz did not want to be too involved and certainly it was not noticed whether she attended the dinners or not. Life was now very different.

She was starting to question and analyse almost everything that was going on in her life and wasn't too sure if it was the life she really wanted anymore. She adored Max that was without question but, now it was a different type of love.

The loving gentleness that Max had been nurturing was not quite so gentle now. Max was so busy with her work these days and never seemed to switch off. The passion and wildness in her painting overflowed into her lovemaking with Liz.

It sometimes scared Liz how powerful Max could be. They needed to talk about it she knew that. Life and love wasn't quite the bed of roses it had been. Despite all the working out that Liz completed daily she knew the inner strength that Max had was far stronger than hers.

Liz was fast becoming withdrawn and rather a solitary figure. She seemed to enjoy being on her own and was not too interested in entertaining or indeed seeing anyone anymore. She had more than enough money in her own right. Since her independence from Sam, her accountants had been very astute with her money and invested very wisely and she was on one of the rich lists in the UK.

Her one aim in life had seemed to be getting fully fit and transforming her body and she now possessed a six pack and had a first class athlete's body. Michael and Sarah who had been her trainers after the accident had become her very close friends and now it was more and more they, who Liz turned to when she needed to talk.

The other three were too engrossed in ensuring that Max would become an international artist to be reckoned with. Very often when Liz had finished in the gym the other three were heavily involved in conversations about exhibitions and when and where to go. Liz thought it odd that they were looking after Max so much as it was Peter who held the strings but she said nothing. In fact sometimes she hardly spoke to any of the others all day.

The days when Liz spent the afternoons leisurely watching Max paint were disappearing fast. She longed for those days again when the two of them would spend time together, talking, laughing and making love – planning their lives together excitedly. They very rarely spent quality time together now.

In fact Liz was very far from alright. She was beginning to question her relationship with the other three. They had always been around her mollycoddling her almost stifling her with their concern and worry. She had distanced herself on purpose and was beginning to analyse everything.

She still wasn't allowed to drive, go horse riding, do any of the things she so loved to do. In the past few years she had felt herself gradually turned into a former vision of herself. Now she began to take herself off into the afternoons to the village. She would walk there through the grounds that she loved and knew so well.

She enjoyed the company of the people at her business in the village in particular the staff at the stables. She was finding her true self again.

A new stable manager had been hired. Liz had been there at the interviews and had immediately taken to the woman who was going to manage her stables. She was not local and had moved up from stables in Newmarket. It had been a unanimous decision by the panel of interviewees to employ Susan.

She was an astute business woman and Liz took to her immediately and over the next few weeks they soon built up a good working relationship and a friendship. She was younger than Liz by about 5 years but very mature for her age. She was confident, good looking and perfect for the job. She was a breath of fresh air to the business and was admired by everyone considering she was 'an outsider'. She was also a breath of fresh air for Liz.

She loved being near the horses again. It was Susan who one day asked why Liz did not ride. Liz explained the situation as they admired the horses in the paddock. Liz personally owned over 20 of them they were fine animals and they were breeding expertly.

Susan saw how sad Liz was at not being able to ride and decided to make some investigations of her own as to why she was not riding. She like being around Liz and the feeling between them was mutual.

It was a shock to her when she found out the truth and vowed to break the news to Liz gently but at the right time. Her enthusiasm for life was captivating. It reminded Liz of how she used to be. She also realised there was no reason now why she too couldn't have the same enthusiasm as she continued to re-evaluate her life.

One afternoon Liz asked what the matter was, why she was so quiet.

"I need to tell you something the staff have all been sworn to secrecy. It's not the hospital that have said you can't ride anymore it's the other three. Certainly for about three years you haven't been allowed to, but in the last year there has not been a reason why you cannot ride. They don't want you too. Liz you need to speak to the hospital yourself, your consultant, I don't want to be responsible for interfering."

There she'd said it. Susan felt as though she was betraying the workforce but her loyalty had to be first to Liz. The woman who had employed her, the woman she was beginning to think more and more about.

At first Liz was unable to speak as she tried to take in what had just been said to her. As she began to take stock of things she then remembered now how Max would always have a private word as she was getting dressed after all her tests.

She realised now that she was leading her life as they wanted her to lead it. She was angry at first then realised that actually her staff were just doing as asked. She always forgave people. She had even forgiven Sam in her own way.

At the end of the day although the business was hers, Mary and Max were the family members who owned most of the land and buildings. They were seen as the rightful owners and the staff would always be loyal to them.

She vowed to speak to her consultant but privately without anyone else knowing. She was beginning to lead her own separate life and was enjoying the freedom. She began to feel the need to spread her wings. She was also beginning to look forward to seeing Susan in the times she was at the business.

As her once perfect relationship with Max began to deteriorate Susan was the one who Liz was talking to about it more, along with Michael and Sarah. They were all becoming concerned as Liz was beginning to rely on them more and more.

Sarah in particular was concerned as she could see something building between Liz and Susan.

Max had flown to Paris with Mary to discuss some finer points with the art gallery. Liz knew deep down she would see Marianne while she was there. At one point she thought about ringing Marianne but it would not be any use.

Max would do whatever Max wanted to do and she just felt that given the right situation she would be with Marianne. She knew that with the state of their relationship anything was possible with Max.

It was becoming common knowledge that Max was travelling without Liz sometimes and the rumours were beginning that perhaps the once so marvellous relationship was teetering. They knew that Max had been with Marianne for several years a long time ago and rumours began to circulate that they had seen each other again.

Liz even asked Max when eventually on their own upon her return if they had met up. Max immediately looked guilty and red in the face and it was then that Liz knew something had happened and yet surprisingly was not desolate.

"Yes we have seen each other Liz," she flared. "But no I have not slept with her if that's what you mean." Max just stared at her with eyes so full of anger as she lied. Much later she hated herself for it. Liz was more frightened than ever of Max.

"Maybe if you had come with me and supported me you would not be asking me such things."

Liz was hurt by the way Max had spoken to her – this seemed to be how it was these days.

Liz knew just by the way Max was that she had seen Marianne. The looks that the two sisters gave each other were enough for her to know something had happened between them.

She didn't know where she stood anymore with Max. She just felt sad that it looked as though this relationship was on its way out. There were now so many rumours going around the village that all was not well in the big house and that Max had seen Marianne.

Even the papers were full of it and there were some pictures of the Max, Mary and Marianne in them. Liz put two and two together. The pair of them kept their distance for a few days. Liz could hardly look at Max. Max would often stay up all night painting as if to avoid being near Liz.

They so needed to talk but Liz felt as though she couldn't be bothered. Her thoughts were more of the stables, her horses, and now Susan. It was not retaliation it was just how life was now.

Eventually the time came when she decided to throw caution to the wind and ride again with strict instructions not to let anyone in the big house know. She had spoken to her consultant quickly. She had her yearly medical approaching so would speak more about it then in the meantime it was a secret only certain members of staff vowed to keep for her as she began to flex her wings. She arrived at the stables one afternoon and announced to Susan she was going to ride.

Together they found some riding clothes. She changed into them at Susan's apartment and Susan could hardly take her eyes off her as she marvelled at the sight of her in the clothes. She looked stunning and Susan wanted her there and then. She made no move though she was too frightened of her feelings for her boss.

It began to scare Liz slightly as up until now she had never even looked at another woman in any other way than as a friend, or colleague. She was frightened because she realised that her own relationship was beginning to fall apart and realised that she needed to speak to Max quickly.

She was becoming attracted to Susan and was nervous. She also knew that she looked good and that Susan's eyes were all over her. If Max or indeed any of them knew what she had been doing there would be a tremendous row, an uproar heaven knows where it would end. She was scared at her feelings and vowed to try to rekindle the relationship that had been so perfect with Max.

Susan lived in an apartment above the stables. The job was her life it was one of the best jobs she had ever had and she certainly did not want to lose the privileges that went with it. She was beginning to have feelings for Liz but knew she was in dangerous waters if she pursued them. Liz would often be in the offices with the other members of staff laughing and chatting and she would look at her in a different way these days. Liz needed to make things right between her and Max before it was too late.

She felt the relationship could be salvaged and she didn't want to give up yet. Yet the way Max treated her made her feel so downtrodden and worthless. Susan saw this and also saw that maybe it was a way into Liz's heart. Liz knew via Rose that Max had cheated on her and felt wretched that Max could not have been honest with her. Maybe they could have worked it out there and then instead of letting it drag on and on.

Liz so wanted things to be right between her and Max but she was beginning to feel it was too late. Max had cheated on her that was all she knew and it hurt but not as much as she thought it would. It was the lying that hurt her the most.

Sarah was no fool and was worried that Liz was becoming attracted to Susan. She knew Liz's relationship was not in the right place and this distraction could prove to be very dangerous. Liz was beginning to grow in confidence and she wondered how much more stifling from the others she was going to endure.

Michael and Sarah knew things were not as they should be and suggested she started to run after her training sessions. They also had to think of their own careers. If something happened between Susan and Liz there would be an outcry. Sarah would have to try to keep Liz on the straight and narrow and she would make it her business to ensure that nothing happened between the two women at least nothing more than had perhaps already happened.

Liz loved the freedom the running gave her. She didn't even know if the others were aware of what she was doing. They were so engrossed with Max. She began to think about her life and the future and where Susan was in the mix of it all.

Liz would spend more and more time with the pair nowadays. They were her confidantes now and she began to rely on them heavily. They had suggested training for marathons and it was this running through the countryside where she could think when she was on her own. Here she could contemplate her life and what she wanted out of it.

Deep down she knew Max had slept with Marianne but that did not give the right to be with Susan or did it – she certainly had feelings for her and the tension between them when they were together was mounting.

Mealtimes, when Liz was there tended to be full of talk about Max's painting and when the next exhibition was unless they were next door entertaining. Liz had up until now fully supported Max in her travelling and had always travelled with her. They had stayed in wonderful hotels which Liz always paid for and she always ensured that Max was looked after well. She had put her life on hold for her and would have gone to the ends of the earth for her at one time.

Now things were different. Liz for once decided she was not going to travel to the next big exhibition. She had made her announcement over the dinner table one night. For once the other three stopped talking and looked at her amazed as what she had just said.

"I just don't want to go this time I have things to do here I need to get on with the book."

Max looked at her slightly hurt and then they all carried on talking. For Liz it had been a huge thing the announcement but they all seemed to take it in their stride. This was Max's biggest moment and yet she had chosen not to go to Paris. She got up from the table unnoticed.

She needed to speak with Max alone, she need to be in her arms to explain why she didn't want to travel so much anymore.

Chapter 7

Liz decided to hold a big party to celebrate the anniversary of the opening of her business. It was towards early summer and all the people who worked for her would be invited. She and a few others from the business plus Michael and Sarah of course would ensure that it was a huge success.

"Plenty of singing and dancing," she said. "I want the happiness back." Her eyes spoke volumes to Sarah of her unhappiness.

It was all arranged and no expense was spared. This would be a huge event, entertainment, and the full works. Liz was in her element as she methodically planned it like she and Sam used to. She had begun to think of the past and Sam far more these days. She had longed for those exciting times again lately. She was thrilled too as she felt she had a purpose in life again. The meeting with the co-writer was due to take place in a few weeks so this in a way was a bit of a swan song as she knew she would not be able to make time at the business for a while as she completed the book – it was her way of saying thank to everyone.

She told them all in the house about the party and realised no one was really listening to her and felt dejected.

"Well it's next week it would be so nice to have some support from you," she said quietly.

No one looked up and it was only when she had gone that Rose realised what she had said. She also noticed that the twins had not even acknowledged her. She thought she would mention it later if they had time, these days they seemed to work at such a frantic pace. Rose was sad as she realised that the once so perfect friendship between them all was disappearing.

With Max the way she was she could be capable of anything. Susan and Liz began to talk about Max and Liz explained that she was often quite scared of her. Nothing could or was going to happen yet deep down she secretly hoped it could. Susan thoroughly understood but she also was getting feelings for Liz. Instead they began to ride out together for several hours at a time in the afternoons. There was a passion growing between them.

Only a few trusted people knew that Liz was riding again and they kept their promises not to let anyone else know. As the weeks went by the attraction was mutual and one day in the stables Susan made her move and kissed Liz. At first Liz backed away saying that it was wrong then relented and kissed her back.

She backed off afterwards

"No this can't happen Susan I need to sort out my relationship."

Susan thoroughly understood and they agreed it must never happen again.

"Anyway we have a party to organise and plan," smiled Liz which seemed to lift the growing tensions.

Everyone was busy with the planning and getting into the party spirit. As the day approached Liz was feeling so happy. She had trained hard in the morning and then went to change for the evening.

As she came downstairs the first thing they noticed was the fact she was dressed in clothes rather than a vest and shorts as she very rarely wore anything else indoors . Her boots made a clipping sound as she came down the stairs. The other three looked as she came down dressed in simple jeans t shirt and leather jacket.

"Going out?" asked Mary.

"Yes it's the anniversary party remember I told you about it last week?" replied Liz not even bothering to look at them.

A guilty feeling came over them all as they realised how far away Liz was from them now in their relationships.

None of them looked as though they were moving as Liz looked around the room sorrowfully.

"Some support would have been nice," she said quietly. "I don't know when I will be back I may stay over."

She turned and left the house.

Michael had driven up to pick her up and as Max looked out of the window she noticed how happy Liz was once she was in the car. She looked at Rose who spoke first.

"I think we all ought to take stock of what is going on here and support Liz."

Max immediately agreed and looked at Mary her eyes telling her sister how sad and worried she was.

"I need to make things right I need to put it right Mary I have let her down so badly."

Rose spoke next.

"Max, Liz knows what happened in Paris."

Mary looked on "Did you tell her?"

"I didn't need to she's not stupid it was all in the papers and look how you have been with her Max, it's as if you are two strangers."

The words took Max back and she tried to pull herself together.

"But just recently we were so happy and celebrating her writing."

Rose looked at her. "Max she's terrified of you and how you might hurt her, you are driving her away with your aggression. We can see what you are doing to her, you need to talk before it is too late. She will go believe me I have seen this look before you are breaking her heart."

Where that came from Rose did not know but the look on Max's face was enough to tell her that she had made her stop and think. Mary was silent.

They began to finish what they were working on quickly and Rose went to the cellar where she ensured they had enough champagne.

Liz arrived with the others and was struck at the carnival atmosphere. It was perfect and everyone was thrilled to see her. It was early and she would soon be making a speech and the festivities would then begin.

She noticed Susan was not there and enquired where she was. On hearing she had been delayed she insisted on returning with her from her apartment. She wanted her there for the speeches she had been so helpful and supportive in the preparations.

She knocked on the door and Susan answered it eventually.

"I'm so sorry I'm running late I won't be long, come in and have a drink." She had showered and was wearing just a towel. Liz tried to ignore the feeling that was growing in her.

Sarah returned dressed similarly to Liz and poured herself a drink too.

"Cheers," she said. "I'm so sorry I was on the phone to another breeder I may have found another horse for you." Her eyes spoke volumes into Liz's.

"Come on," said Liz, "let's go we've got a long night of partying we can talk about it tomorrow," as she stopped herself from moving any closer to her.

They left together minutes later and Sarah above all was happy to see them so quickly after Liz had gone to collect her. She knew the attraction was building between them. She watched as they walked from the stable chatting and laughing and began to feel a niggle of concern. If things progressed any further there would be trouble she knew it. She was also worried about their jobs too. If something went wrong between Liz and Max heaven knows where they would end up.

The party was in full swing it was about 10 pm and Liz was having the time of her life. There was dancing, singing, entertainment all sorts and she looked around yes this was a party they would all remember. She looked at Sarah enjoying herself and once or twice their eyes met.

The evening was a huge success and the atmosphere was electric. Liz was boiling hot after they had all danced and went outside for some fresh air. She walked away from the noise for five minutes as she made her ways to her beloved stables. There were people milling about everywhere all saying what wonderful night it had been.

"Here," said Susan, "I've brought you a drink it's so hot in there."

Liz gratefully took the drink she was parched. Susan looked at Liz wanting her more than anything else in the world and took her hand.

"Come on," she whispered as Liz moved towards her.

She put her arm on her shoulder and kissed her. Liz broke away and then Susan took her hand again

"You know you want to," she whispered.

Liz didn't know what she wanted anymore she just knew at that moment she wanted to be held by someone.

Susan went towards her and kissed her again this time there was no rejection. She held Liz tightly and kissed her longingly her tongue exploring her mouth. Liz responded and realised she was enjoying this woman.

"Come on," said Rose to Max, "hurry up."

They had all changed and were going to support Liz in the venue. As they drove down to the village Max asked them to stop. They had crates of drink in the boot and were now looking forward to a party.

"Let me just walk the last few hundred yards its ages since I have been here I want to take it all in."

"What's wrong Liz? Don't deny you have feelings for me I can see it in your eyes," Susan said softly.

Liz then kissed her back feeling her passion rising in her body. Susan's hands began to explore the rest of Liz's body as they both began to caress each other. Susan kissed her neck as Liz responded urgently. As their passion mounted they both realised what was going to happen.

"Let's go to my place," said Susan breathlessly as she led Liz in the dark round to her door. Liz went with her and once inside their hands and mouths were everywhere on each other. They began to undo each other's clothes frantically as they began to explore each other's bodies.

They stopped abruptly as they heard Sarah calling for Liz through the door.

"Hey I was getting worried." She had seen them walk round the back of the stables and wanted to prevent a disaster. "Is everything ok?"

Liz was relieved and yet appalled at what she had done. She had never looked at another woman before but she was being driven away slowly by the others and Max.

"This must never happen again Susan, do you understand." She looked straight into her eyes.

"Of course, I'm so sorry Liz." She looked forlorn but thoroughly understood.

The three of them went back to the party but the spark had been ignited and Sarah knew in time that something would happen between them and probably tonight as she did not think that Liz would go home. Susan wanted Liz with a burning passion.

They all went back into the hall and were talking to everyone. The room was so full of people no one except Sarah had noticed they had been missing for about ten minutes. Suddenly the room went quiet. Liz turned round and there in the middle of the room was Max.

"Hey," she said looking at Liz, "sorry we're late."

She went straight up to Liz and kissed her in front of everyone. She had seen Liz and Susan together with Sarah. She had seen the way Susan was looking at Liz.

She knew she had to win Liz's heart and the way to win it back was to be the gentle woman that Liz had fallen in love with all those years ago.

She indulged her with anything she could that night and gave Susan a look once or twice that spelt volumes. If Susan wanted to keep her job she needed to keep her hands off the woman she was going to marry.

The party was a huge success and during the rest of the evening Liz ensured that she and Susan spoke about what had almost happened. They both apologised and were both determined it would not affect their working relationship. It would be a tough call and in a way Liz was pleased that for the next few weeks she would not be able to spend so much time in the village due to the writing of the book. They both agreed to talk the next day about it but for now they were to enjoy what was left of the evening. Sarah had hardly left their side and was relieved when it looked as though it was all something they had to forget.

It was late when eventually Liz and Max left for home. The other two had left an hour or so earlier. Max was there to support and made sure she never let Liz out of her sight. She wasn't sure if anything had happened between the two of them and she realised it was her fault that Liz had had her head turned by someone else.

She needed to make things better now, and began to think of ways she could. She hated herself for having betrayed her partner and vowed to make it right between them she also knew she should confess all to Liz but not tonight.

They walked slowly back to the big house. Once home she held Liz in her arms telling her how much she loved her and how sorry she was for how she had treated her. Once inside as usual Liz fell for Max's charms questioning nothing. Max began to kiss her longingly and as her hands began to undress her Liz allowed her to do whatever she wanted with her. Max knew how to tantalize and tease Liz and soon the pair of them were in bed fondling and caressing each other.

They were both expert lovers and knew exactly how to excite each other. They were so in tune with each other when Max was in the right frame of mind, they both cried out in ecstasy as they fulfilled each other again and again. Liz was in heaven as her Max seemed to have returned to the Max she had fallen in love with all those years ago, the caring loving Max.

It was late the next day when they both woke Max looking decidedly the worse for wear. Liz never suffered from hangovers as she rarely drank. She decided to go for a run while Max pulled herself together.

"I'll be a couple of hours," she said kissing Max. "Go back to sleep you'll feel better."

After showering she went off for a run having made a call first. She met up with Susan who had ridden to a spot where they would often ride to and they sat and talked about what happened the night before.

"I really do want you Liz you must know that." Susan's eyes pleaded with her.

"I have never been unfaithful to anyone," she replied.

Susan took her hand she was so forlorn as Liz carried on speaking.

"I know Max can change," she replied.

It wasn't enough to convince Susan as she went to kiss her again. Liz went to back off again but Susan held her closer she was not giving up this time.

"You know you want to Liz you know you want me as much as I want you."

Liz looked at her and a host of thoughts went through her mind. Max had cheated on her she knew that. She was so violent with her sometimes; she had driven her into the arms of another woman.

They were a fair way away from the business and it was a wonderfully warm summer's afternoon with the sun shining brightly on them. Liz simply looked at Susan her eyes filling with tears as she realised how close she was now to being unfaithful.

"No Susan go back, this must not happen," she was trying desperately not to give in to temptation.

At that moment at that time she wanted her more than anything else but she knew it was so wrong. Susan untethered the horse and began to walk back but as she went she gave Liz one final look which spoke volumes.

Liz then turned away and began to walk back home. After a few steps she stopped and looked back again, Susan was still looking at her – she walked towards Susan as they made their way back to the stables in silence there was no need for words. At the stables Susan gave the horse to a stable girl to unsaddle.

They made their way to the apartment trying to act normally and professionally and not give reason for anyone to speculate on what might happen between them. They climbed the stairs and Susan opened the door. Once inside they looked at each other both scared and excited and desperate for each other.

Susan moved towards Liz and kissed her so tenderly as she whispered

"I want you so much."

Liz looked at her and responded with a passionate kiss.

"Then take me now," she replied huskily as they made their way to the bedroom.

This time they were not interrupted as Susan removed their clothes. She began to kiss Liz all over her body gently and passionately as her hands explored everywhere. Her tongue tantalised Liz.

Liz had no other thoughts other than to please Susan and be pleasured herself as they slowly and carefully made love. Not once did she think about Max and what she was doing with Susan. She completely gave herself unselfishly to Susan as they took each other again and again to the limits of their passion. Afterwards they lay there silently. The last few hours had been a culmination of a build-up of emotions and tension. Liz knew Susan had feelings for her but she did not really know where she was mentally herself. She began to cry quietly and it was Susan who spoke first.

"I know," she said gently as she caressed her back. She knew exactly where she stood with her and although she knew she had fallen in love with her, Liz would never feel the same as long as she was with Max.

"Don't feel guilty, it has happened and we need to put it behind us Liz." This made Liz feel better and more relaxed.

After about an hour they agreed that nothing like that must ever take place again. They both decided it was for the best and that spending some time apart while Liz completed the book would be helpful. Eventually Susan agreed and realised that Liz was right. She was mad to have thought that anything could progress from this. Liz adored Max but Susan made it plain that if ever anything did happen between her and Max she would be there for her. There was now a bond between them.

Liz showered, she had to get back as she had been longer than she should. She slipped out of the apartment and was pleased no one had seen her. No one except Max. Max had walked to the village to try to find Liz as she had been away too long. She had seen how they had looked at each other the night before and knew something would happen between them. She would not mention it but it would plague her for a while as she came to terms with the fact they had both now cheated on each other.

Yes thought Liz on her way home her personality had altered since the accident. She knew up until now she was not the person she once was. She was no longer vibrant and exciting, she had turned into someone she did not recognise. She was not her own person any more. She almost had to get permission to do anything different these days. She needed her own space where she could think.

Now, however she vowed to change and be her own person again as she used to be. Her whole body and emotions had been reawakened by someone other than Max. She needed to find Max and speak about everything before things got out of hand. She didn't hate herself for what she had just done she just felt confused.

Chapter 8

Max knew Liz had seemed to be more withdrawn since their return from America, she had enjoyed the feeling of space over there. Her days now were very solitary in a way. She would work out in the morning. She was obsessed on the exercise and looked forward to it every day. Sarah and Michael had fast become her main friend and confidantes.

Liz would often spend evenings with them planning charity events. They had encouraged her to start running and they were working on some charity runs for brain damaged people. There was talk of marathons, she was beginning to live a life that did not always include the other three.

When the workout was completed she often tried to spend time with Max in her studio. That was not the same now. Max was in huge demand and she would often be with Mary and Rose while they planned exhibitions, tours, interviews. Peter who was now their publicist would arrange even more exhibitions. To being with after the return from America Liz would accompany her to these exhibitions but now it began to clash with her exercise, her life.

She was obsessed with it nothing could get in her way. The once vibrant exciting woman that Liz was was now becoming quieter and she just wanted the easier life. She had done all the travelling before she and Max got together, now she was looking at settling down more. She had a routine which she loved it was now her life.

"Settle down," cried Max, "you are not even forty yet you have your whole life ahead of you let's enjoy it." she sounded almost frightened that Liz maybe did not want the same exciting life as she did.

The physical side of their relationship was changing too. Whenever Max had pressure on her for whatever reason the relationship changed. It became urgent tempestuous hard and fast. Now it did not suit Liz so much, she wanted the gentleness that Max had been nurturing. The tactile relationship from Liz's point of view had also changed. Max was the one who was under pressure now and Liz just began to accept things for what they were.

She became withdrawn and quiet as she felt she could not and would not speak to Max while she was like this. Perhaps in hindsight she though much later they should have talked more instead of just hiding behind the truth – the truth that the once so perfect love affair was not quite so perfect anymore.

Liz had her yearly medical at the hospital in Inverness approaching and the publishers wanted her to meet their co-writer. Liz and Max both agreed that to meet in Inverness would be less daunting than at the house so they arranged both appointments for two consecutive days. The hospital appointment usually took the best part of the day with gruelling tests and exercises and Liz usually felt quite tired afterwards.

Max as ever would ensure that Liz was by her side. For the past few years she had personally seen to it that Liz never overdid anything. It was as if Liz was a china doll that could be broken if dropped, in actual fact it could not be further from the truth. Liz was now beginning to question her life and what the future held for it. This was the reason she was becoming withdrawn she was in fact taking stock of her life.

Max took over immediately. Since their return from America Liz had not really travelled anywhere to talk of so this would be a lovely treat. Money was absolutely no object they had nothing to lose. She would spoil her.

"We could book a suite and really enjoy ourselves, pamper each other," said Max now gently but slightly excited.

Max knew herself that things were not right between them. She knew that something was troubling Liz but she was so caught up in her work she just kept avoiding it.

Her feelings for Liz had not changed she still adored her and would go to the ends of the world for her. She would ensure that Liz never did anything she shouldn't, would never overdo things but she had her own life to think about now. Her career had taken off and she knew Liz was somehow being left behind. She also felt guilty about the time she had spent with Marianne. She knew Liz had been with Susan on that afternoon and she felt wretched, she had to make things right between them again.

They had both been unfaithful and yet neither had spoken about it she just knew she wanted Liz and wanted to be with her forever. Marianne had been a huge mistake. She thought about her as she planned things in her head for Liz.

Max had wanted her to travel with her but Liz eventually decided she did not want to live out of a suitcase. When they first got together they never spent any time apart. Now Max would travel with Mary or Rose when there were interviews, exhibitions and openings to attend. Sometimes the break did them good and when they got back together it was like the old times when they couldn't keep their hands off each other. Liz had her world and she had hers.

She had met up with Marianne several times in Paris and each time they had slept together. It was wonderful to see her again and be in her world. Nothing had happened between them at first until their emotions got the better of them. Marianne had kissed Max one night unexpectedly.

They would always have a bond yet Marianne had taken advantage of a situation. Max had been talking about Liz and how things weren't as they should be. Instead of listening she did the unforgivable and made a play for her. Max looked at her eyes wild with anger an anger Marianne had never seen before.

There was an anger that was brewing inside Max. Marianne was alarmed at this and wondered how many times she got into such a rage, she apologised for her actions immediately to try to calm Max down.

"Come back to mine and we can talk."

Forlornly Max went back to the flat where they began to talk and drink. As they got drunker and smoked more she relaxed and this time as Marianne kissed her again she responded.

After all these years it was as if they had never been apart as they took each other to insatiable limits. Hours later as they lay in silence Max realised she had betrayed her Liz – this would not be the first and only time and hated herself.

This anger would build and build dangerously as she hid the truth from Liz. Liz almost knew immediately when she returned what had happened she sensed it.

"Oh Max that would be wonderful – just the two of us how lovely," replied Liz as she looked into Max's eyes almost relieved that they could be alone together with no interruptions.

Max had at last begun to notice over the past few weeks how quiet again Liz was becoming so she was determined to pull out all of the stops – just the two of them. She had listened to what Rose had said and vowed to put things right.

She also knew that Liz had slept with Susan. They could be together and try to put everything into a better situation than the one they were in. There had never been any question of unfaithfulness until now it was just that their lives were so different.

They arranged to meet Jaime who was to be the co-writer the following morning and make arrangements about the writing process and have some lunch together. They would then have the afternoon and evening together and then travel to the hospital for the late morning appointment the next day. Liz could then sleep on the hour long journey home. Max would ensure Liz would not overdo anything. If anything Max was almost too controlling, stifling her with concern.

Liz was beginning to feel hemmed in and knew the situation would have to be sorted out it was as though she couldn't do anything on her own without seeking approval. It was almost as if there was nothing in her life that was spontaneous anymore unless she was with Susan

"We could always really push the boat out and have two nights in the city," laughed Liz.

"Why not. We can do what we want for the rest of our lives," exclaimed Max as she booked it excitedly. This would mean they would not have to rush back after the hospital.

She looked into her eyes they were so troubled and full of worry. Yes they desperately needed this time together they could put things right she was sure. She couldn't imagine life without Liz she couldn't lose her now not after everything they had been through.

She planned to ask Liz to be her civil partner and this was her opportunity when they would be alone together. She was so sure she could make things right and she desperately did not want to lose her. Whether this was the right time to ask her she didn't know she just did not want to lose Liz.

"You can tell Mary," she replied smiling almost with relief that they were going to be on their own for a few days.

"She's not that bad," said Max. "She just does what she thinks is best. She just loves organising me and always has done she feels responsible for me. She will never change its just the way we are."

Max would always support her sister and she would always in the end find the good in her. Liz on the other hand had no siblings to form that sort of bond with.

"I know it's just it would be better coming from you," sighed Liz

It was true she was becoming more of a recluse but it was because she wanted to be with Max more and not constantly have Rose and Mary around. She wanted things back to how they were but deep down knew that it was impossible. Mary continued to interrupt at some rather awkward moments and this was affecting their relationship. They had always been a very tactile couple but sometimes with them all working and spending most of the day in their part of the house it was all becoming rather oppressive.

Their lives were not the same as before. She questioned whether it was because of what had happened five years ago or whether they were beginning to drift apart. Max was in demand all over the world. Up until a few months ago Max had refused to travel anywhere else in the world since their return from America, but Liz knew sooner or later Max would want to travel abroad to all of the exhibitions which were being planned it was her destiny.

Liz wasn't so sure whether or not she wanted to spend the next few months travelling. She loved being at home training and working out in the gym and seeing her staff in the village that she was fast becoming so popular with. It seemed their preferences in life were beginning to differ. She just hoped that their relationship wasn't changing too much to be salvaged. They both knew the other had cheated, they were both desolate if only they could talk about it make it better. Whenever Max was either preparing for an exhibition or painting a commissioned piece their relationship changed. It became more urgent desperate and sometimes Liz found it difficult to keep up it was becoming a strain sometimes.

It was almost like Max still had to get approval from her sister.

"If you think you can spare two days away from your important work then go," Mary muttered.

She was once again crestfallen that the four of them were not going to go together. There always a downside these days to anything Max and Liz wanted to do.

"Well we're going and that's that. Anyway it'll do you and Rose good to be together on your own. Rose doesn't seem herself," replied Max.

"She's fine she's just tired," and she turned and went back to her work.

Liz also seemed concerned about Rose. Often before they would go for a long walk and talk. Max knew how they liked to talk together privately away from Mary. She never minded and in fact would often suggest Liz talked to Rose. Max had grown very fond of Rose over the years but she also agreed she did not seem herself.

"Come on Rose, talk to me what's wrong?" asked Liz one day.

Rose insisted that there was nothing but her eyes spoke another story.

"Is it you and Mary? Please tell me." Liz was so concerned for her friend.

"I'm ok just got things on my mind that's all," lied Rose.

In fact she was fast becoming quite good at lying. She certainly did have things on her mind the civil ceremony (Max had told Rose and Mary what she planned to ask Liz) and Liz's 40th were all this year and that was just the beginning...

She and Mary were reasonably happy – their relationship was not in the right place at all but maybe it could be salvaged. It would never be the relationship that Rose had been searching for all her life. It just suited.

"What can I do to help? I cannot bear to see you like this." Liz was becoming upset – it was obvious to Rose.

Liz so wanted everyone to be happy and in love everything was seen out of her tinted coloured glasses. Rose just looked gave Liz a hug and told another lie to try to pacify Liz.

"Maybe I'm just over emotional perhaps it's my age," replied Rose as she managed to put on a false grin and laughed.

Rose was one of Liz's dearest friends and she hated to see her like this but Rose somehow had managed to convince her that all was well. In fact Rose was far from alright her biggest secret had after all these years come back to haunt her.

Chapter 9

Liz was so excited as she packed a few items. They were going to the city, the bright lights; see other people, she couldn't wait. She never complained about how she was feeling these days maybe she should have. America had been amazing and although the four of them were together there just seemed to be so much space between them over there.

Liz still did not drive and probably never would again. Max had decided that. Max put the bags in the back of the car and pretended not to notice Liz as she shut her eyes and took a deep breath as if to say freedom. She knew how she felt and sooner or later the problem especially with Mary would have to be addressed.

Max would be the first to agree that she and Liz needed time together. Yes she was concerned about Rose and Mary but she was far more concerned about her and Liz. She knew deep down her sister was driving a wedge between them all and it needed to stop. Maybe that was why Rose seemed a bit down and distracted.

"Enjoy yourselves and just don't overdo anything tomorrow Liz needs to get through the hospital tests the next day. Don't keep her up all-night," Rose almost sounded as if she was giving out an order.

There she'd said it. It was a very unlike Rose to make comment but she now worried so much about her dearest friend. Max gave her a strange look she was very fond of Rose and thought it a strange remark to make. It was also rather a personal comment very unusual from the prim and proper Rose.

The drive into Inverness was quiet to begin with. Liz was taking in the scenery and just trying to relax. She knew at the moment that Max was in fine form and in a good mood. She had taken time out from her painting for Liz and she loved her for that.

Gradually they began to talk about mundane things both knowing that deep down things were far from right between them and yet neither of them knew where to start. They both knew they had cheated on each other yet chose not to discuss it, another mistake.

The drive took just over the hour, and during that time they began to slowly relax talking and laughing together enjoying each other's company. Things were going back to how they used to be thought Liz as they checked into the very expensive and exclusive hotel. They were immediately recognised by some paparazzi but they were very kind to them and gave them their privacy.

They wanted an interview with Max and Liz together. The two women agreed but it would be when they were ready later in the day they had their own agenda to keep to. The first priority was to meet the co-writer that Liz would be working with. Their bags were taken to their suite as they had no time before their lunch appointment.

Jaime was waiting for them in the lounge with her agent. The two women took to her immediately and they enjoyed a good but light lunch. Max noticed how Liz picked her way through her salad but said nothing while they ironed out some ground rules. Liz wanted the book to be as truthful as possible and it would also mean talking in great lengths to Rose, Max and Mary along with some close friends of Liz.

Mad did not realise that Liz was beginning to dread the evening. She knew that Max would drink too much and probably become hurtful towards her, she was becoming anxious about it but again said nothing.

They gave Jaime a copy of the diary so that she could begin to acclimatise herself to the four of them and what had happened all those years ago with Sam.

"No need," she said, "I have already got a copy to read. This book will be amazing. It will give so much hope to people who have suffered brain injuries and the recovery they can make. I have already made a start on it so will bring everything with me when we start."

Jaime was a lovely lady who had been writing for many years. She had been quite successful in her own right and now there was the opportunity to co-write with Liz on a book that unknown to the two of them would prove to be so successful and provide them with added financial rewards.

Her past was nothing to write home about she had been married no children. The marriage had not survived and she eventually decided after a few relationships to throw herself into writing. She was thrilled when she got the call from the publishers and even more excited when she realised who she would be writing with. She was friendly and unassuming and Max and Liz both liked her immediately. They knew she would fit in at home with the other two women and they began to look forward to a new chapter in their lives.

Chapter 10

They were all excited and Max was so full of support for Liz. Liz had supported her with her painting and always been there for her so this was the least she could do for Liz. She was so proud of her and how far she had come since that dreadful time with Sam when she had hurt her to the point of near death.

Max had thought long and hard about these few days away and was concentrating on making Liz feel as though she was the most important person in the world again. She knew she had ignored her and hurt her. Max would never forgive Sam for the damage she caused and if she ever met her she would not be responsible for her actions. She felt her anger raging inside her every time she thought about that terrible time. Max above all had found it the hardest to forget that day. She had watched her partner have the life beaten out of her which in turn had changed their whole relationship.

Liz on the other hand would always end up forgiving people whatever their transgressions had been. She wondered if she had forgiven Sam. She realised they hadn't talked about anything recently in any great depth. She didn't know what Liz was thinking anymore.

Even now when Max thought about it her temper started to boil. For years she had managed to restrain herself and her temper but these days with the pressure being put on her it was becoming harder and harder to curtail it.

She knew when the pressure was fully on that she treated Liz differently. She was more aggressive in her behaviour towards her. She had never been knowingly violent but everything just seemed so deep nowadays, she felt she just could not stop herself.

She had helped nurse Liz back to health but never had as much therapy as the others. She was strong and had felt that she could overcome the terrible time of events. She managed to keep her temper under control but it was sometimes difficult when she saw Liz struggling over something as simple as tying up a shoe lace.

Most of the time she managed to control it but she was aware at how near the edge she was sometimes. She knew deep down she needed some help but her life was too busy. Yes her life, she realised now how separate they had become she was thinking of her life and not their life – there really was a problem.

After a long lunch Jaime left looking forward to when they would begin working on the book. Max and Liz then agreed to give the paparazzi a short interview. They especially adored Max considering her to be the local hero and the short piece would be in the paper the day after tomorrow.

The interview lasted about an hour and satisfied that the article was suitable, they went to the suite for the first time.

Liz realised when they went through the door that this must be one of the most expensive suites in the hotel. Max had for once booked it ensuring they had only the best it was gorgeous and Liz immediately began to take in the views from the large window as Max began to unpack.

They were on the 15th floor so they had a wonderful outlook over the city. They both began to relax as Max opened some champagne. It had been a long time since the two of them had been totally alone. Max looked at her and then held her at first gently and then more tightly as they slowly began to become aroused with each other.

"I want things back to how they used to be," she whispered as Liz responded to her touch.

It was the one thing that Liz wanted in life but she felt things were never going to be the same again

"I was thinking," she said as she kissed her neck. "How about doing some shopping later on?"

"Do we need anything?" replied Liz softly; she was just thrilled to be in her lover's arms.

"I thought we ought to be thinking of some wedding rings." There she'd said it.

It was probably the wrong time, they needed to have spent more time together before she asked her. Liz looked at her as her eyes filled. Max had practiced so many times on how to ask her and yet here she was very casually in the end asking the biggest question in her life.

"I mean," she stuttered slightly, "I mean… well what… I mean is will you marry me? I know things have not been as they should be lately and I know it's my fault but I know we can fix it. I want us to get things back to how they were."

Liz looked at her lovingly, knowing deep down that this was what Max wanted more than anything else in the world. And very, very quietly whispered in her ear

"You know I will my darling." Not sure if she was doing the right thing or not – another mistake.

They held each other for what seemed like ages both of them hoping deep down they could mend their relationship. They drank the champagne not too much for Liz, those days were long gone she only drank now and again.

The other three continued to drink quite heavily though and Max gave up smoking soon after she met Liz. It was only when she was with Marianne that she continued to smoke. Max took Liz by the hand and gently led her to the vast bedroom.

She began slowly and gently to undress Liz and began to kiss her softly. Max ensured that she treated Liz with the utmost gentleness as she knew sometimes she was too rough with her. She began to kiss her body tenderly showing her just how gentle she could be. This was how it should be thought Liz as she began to respond to Max voluntarily for the first time in ages. Her body quivered as Max kissed her everywhere. The past indiscretions were forgotten for the time being as they fulfilled each other.

Her hands began to caress Liz as she too was undressed by Liz. What had begun as slow and tentative now began to speed up as they both began to fulfil each other with hands and tongues. They both cried out again and again in ecstasy as at last their bodies were in tune with each other.

Afterwards it was Max who spoke first. She looked into Liz's eyes

"This is how we should be Liz I know I have not treated as I should have done."

Liz looked at her and saw the concern in her eyes.

"Shh," she whispered, "let's just enjoy what we have and they work on putting things right."

For several hours they took each other to the ultimate point of ecstasy trying to erase any concerns they both had until exhausted they fell into a satisfied sleep.

Max woke first and looked at Liz sleeping. She kissed her shoulder and marvelled at her body as she looked at the way Liz had transformed it to a wonderful shape. The sight of her aroused Max again as she began to kiss her but gently not how she did when she was engulfed in the pressure of her painting. Again they fulfilled each other crying out in sheer ecstasy. It was as if they had been apart for a very long time which in fact they had. They had been too distant with each other for too long.

Later Max then excitedly decided they would go and chose some rings. They had plans to make, the ceremony, where to hold it who to invite.

"Slow down Max we have plenty of time," smiled Liz as she relaxed more and more.

Max had for a split second reverted back to the spontaneous free spirited unthinking Max who charged into everything at a fast and furious rate.

Instead of going to a jeweller they had the jewellers come to their suite. They were sworn to secrecy but eventually they agreed on a handmade pair of rings encrusted with diamonds.

They went for dinner talking nonstop trying to work out where things had gone wrong and yet not really talking about the things that mattered. Max realised she was to blame and kept on repeating to Liz how she would change, how things would be better. They ordered more champagne. It was probably too much for Liz but they threw caution to the wind as if they were naughty school girls.

Naturally they paid for it the next day and they were both thankful that they had the whole day to recover before the next day's appointment at the hospital. They spent the day together carrying on as if nothing was wrong hiding their true feelings from each other.

Max rung Mary and Rose and Liz rang Peter, Michael and Sarah and later Susan. They agreed to let the news out to the press as it was decided it would do Max's career some good to be settling down and getting married.

The rest of the day was spent leisurely sightseeing and a meal then an early night they were both exhausted. And there was the hospital the next day. Max ensured Liz was cared for and well looked after all day as she used to do.

The usual tests went on and on and exhausted Liz. Although she was exceptionally fit it was still as usual something of a strain for her. Throughout the afternoon her memories came flooding back about what she remembered about the accident as they always did. She had been quickly made unconscious by the blows wielded on her by Sam which in a way was a blessing as she could not remember everything that had been done to her. Her results were good but not as good as hoped.

"I think you have been overdoing it a bit, just slowdown there is no rush. You are almost 40 and have the rest of your life. You have a personal trainer so maybe he can slow things down a bit. Do you want me to speak to him? After all it was me that put him in touch with you." Her specialist was slightly concerned about her mental and physical condition.

"Yes ok it would be easier coming from you. I think if you spoke to him. Can you also tell Max about the riding?"

She just had to let Max know that she would be riding again – she would pick her moment even though she had secretly been riding lately another secret she had kept. They were fast becoming good at keeping things from each other.

Chapter 11

As soon as possible after her return from the hospital five years ago, Liz had thrown herself into the gym determined to repair her body. It was her specialist who had mentioned a personal trainer and Michael was hired who put her through her structured paces.

He was a giant of a man with muscles on top of muscles. He had moved to the village with his wife Sarah and occasionally at the beginning his wife would train too. Now she was regularly working out with Liz. Michael had been a personal trainer in Inverness for about six years. He owned his own gym having poured nearly all of his savings into it. It had thrived and he was on the point of opening a new gym when he met Sarah. He immediately was attracted to her and within days of meeting they were an item. They were married within a year both running the two gyms within months of their marriage. They were a popular couple in the fitness world and were delighted when they had a call asking them if they would be interested in helping Liz after her release from hospital.

Originally they were to spend one or two mornings a week at the house in the Highlands but as time and Liz's energy returned it soon became apparent that they were needed full time. Liz and the pair developed a very strong friendship very quickly and she was very generous in her recognition of their loyalty and friendship.

She paid for them to live on the estate and eventually they became her personal assistants and would in time be her closest allies in what was to become. As time went on Liz had a large gym built in the village premises which ensured that the rest of the staff could work out with Michael and Sarah. She also thought it would do her good to be away from the house – she was spending more and more time away from the others now. She would train mostly in the village. She would run there in the morning and then on her way back. She was also spending more and more time at the stables.

Sarah had trained as a nurse rising through the ranks quickly and was highly qualified. Liz got on with them both very well and a special bond began to be formed between the three of them. This bond would prove to be unconditional in time to come. Max thoroughly approved of the couple and the four in the early years would sometimes meet up for a drink in the village. This proved to be such a relief for Liz who was feeling more and more stifled by their lifestyle.

Back at the hospital Liz exclaimed, "I know but it's not like I'm 20 again is it?" For once she had made a comment about her age. Time was catching up and yet she felt wonderful she looked fit and lithe…

"Don't get me wrong the tests are good but you are physically tired just take it a bit easier. Is there something on your mind you seem distracted." Her specialist was now delving deep into her mind.

She began to open up about her relationship with Max and spent over an hour past her appointment time talking about it. It was good for her to open up and afterwards she felt so much better. Max worried she had been so long.

In fact they were thrilled with her results but she needed to stop trying to prove to everyone she was superwoman. They also let Max know that Liz knew she could ride again. It was easier coming from them Liz thought. They were very tactful and ensured that Max thoroughly understood how much progress Liz had made.

They drove back home from the hotel quietly. Liz was slightly disappointed.

"Well I suppose we asked for that maybe four hours in the gym every day is too much. And then there is the running just slow down a bit," Max said quietly she was so concerned for Liz. "Just don't go everyday your body is in great shape just chill a bit. Anyway you're going to need all your strength with the planning of our ceremony."

She was jealous of the amount of time Liz spent in the gym and at the stables especially with Susan. She would put a stop to that she thought angrily.

"Max do you really think I am going to be able to do any of the planning with Rose and Mary taking over?" She laughed gingerly.

Max looked at her, Liz was right they hadn't had a hope of planning anything like this on their own.

"Do you mind though if they takeover you know what they're like," asked Max.

"No of course not but maybe they could do some work in their part of the house rather than in ours. We need to be able to spend more time on our own Max like we just have done. I can't see a happy future for us at this rate," and she began to cry quietly.

Liz realised they had both got caught up in the excitement and had forgotten perhaps the problems they had between them. Having had a couple of days away on their own it was now in this hour that they began to talk about things which should have been spoken about much much earlier. The last couple of nights had been like a dream they had indulged each other but not really spoken at length about their relationship.

They had skimmed the surface of the problems as they were beginning to get caught up in the excitement of the forthcoming ceremony. They both knew they had cheated and yet were frightened to talk about it. At one time they would have both been devastated but things were different now between them.

Max stopped the car and switched the engine off.

Although they were so excited about the forthcoming ceremony they both agreed that their relationship was beginning to alter. She looked at Liz and held her for what seemed like ages and kissed her passionately longingly and gently.

"Right I'll tell you what we're going to do," said Max rather forthrightly and breathlessly.

They were about twenty minutes into the journey. She picked up her mobile and rang the hotel back. She turned the car round and they drove back to Inverness. Liz looked at her and realised that Max was as concerned as she was about their relationship. They desperately needed this time on their own even if it was just to talk. They began to laugh nervously and then gradually relax again as they hurtled back.

Max quickly rang home and explained they were having a few extra days that everything was fine they just wanted some time together. Liz rang Michael and Sarah.

"Great stuff," said Michael. "Enjoy yourselves and congratulations." He looked at Sarah they thought perhaps now everything would be ok.

Chapter 12

Max and Liz talked and talked about what was happening in their lives and how they could repair their relationship. It was the first time they had spoken so frankly for a long time. Max was too nervous to bring the subject up and Liz well she just didn't want to upset Max as she was working so hard getting ready for an exhibition in Paris later that year.

It was almost cathartic for them both to be so honest. They eventually mentioned the fact they had been unfaithful. They both cried as they were truthful with each other both of them apologising yet not blaming each other. They accepted what had happened and vowed to put it behind them – they promised.

Liz talked about how their relationship seemed strained whenever Max had an event coming up and how she almost dreaded the bedroom activities sometimes due to Max's force. Max was terribly upset but Liz had said it.

"Why didn't you say something?" she wailed.

Liz explained that for all these years Max had looked after her and she felt it almost her duty to repay her by giving in to her on these occasions.

"Duty," she almost spat the word out, "what do you mean duty how could you say that?"

Liz watched as the temper that Max had controlled for so long belong to bubble over. She checked herself and took a deep breath and then calmed down.

Max was beside herself with sadness as she watched the woman of her dreams break down in front of her. She had done this she had brought her to this situation with her greed and determination to get to the top of the tree in the art world. She did not realise the severity of how much she changed under pressure. Liz carried on

"I see it in your eyes Max. I see the fire when you are painting and then you can't switch off you carry on at this pace which frightens me sometimes, I think one day you are going to hurt me so much." Tears were beginning to form and now flowed freely.

The happiness of a few hours ago had disappeared as things took a very serious turn.

"You broke my heart when you lied about Marianne. It was the lying Max that hurt me so much I knew you had slept together yet you could not look at me and tell me."

Max was desperately upset and held her so closely apologising promising she would change.

"Remember how you were so gentle? You were nurturing that gentleness Max, but now I don't know where I am with you sometimes. I love you so much and yet you are not the person I fell in love with. Our lives have changed forever but we need to remember each other. I feel as if I am on a rollercoaster and I cannot get off." Liz was now crying desperately.

Max was devastated. She immediately held Liz as she cried and cried. At last Liz could explain how she felt it was such a relief as the tears flowed easily now. The hospital had unearthed the feelings that needed to be discussed.

"I'm so sorry please we need to talk about this and make things right again." cried Max.

She was panicking now as Liz seemed to be hyperventilating. They had both admitted they had slept with other people which hurt them both as they now openly talked about it.

She held her as if she would not let her go. Liz continued to sob gently until gradually Max managed to get her to stop. They broke away from each other and then sat in the large suite talking for a long time about how they would make things right. Max moved closer to Liz and began to hold her gently as Liz carried on talking.

Liz allowed herself to be held by Max. Max was so scared of losing her.

"Please Liz let me try again let me love you again let things go back to how they were I love you so much."

Liz had heard it all before she just hoped Max could control herself and her temper.

"I love you Max, but not when you hurt me when you take me you frighten me," Liz replied.

"Liz I saw you almost die in front of me I would never knowingly hurt you I love you please let us start again and make it right." Max was beside herself with worry now.

Max who for so long had appeared strong began to crumple. She knelt in front of Liz with the head on her lap. She sobbed, and sobbed, begging Liz to forgive her.

Eventually hours later Max took Liz to the bedroom and began to show her the gentleness and tenderness that had been missing for some time. She showered Liz with kisses and gentleness as she allowed Liz to relax more. Liz was so tired and yet she knew how important this night was for them both.

Yet again she allowed Max to love her, yet again she responded and finally succumbed to her. Nothing had changed really. They fell asleep Liz not quite sure if they had really made any headway in the repair of their relationship.

A long time afterwards they talked about Paris and decided that the two of them would stay on after the exhibition on their own and have a break – maybe a delayed honeymoon. Maybe have Christmas out there it would be a celebration of Liz's 40th.

"We'll never get away with that," replied Liz sad that it was only now that Max was thinking about just the two of them.

"If not Paris then where? We can go anywhere we want Max."

"I know we can," she replied. "As long as it's not too remote I have to keep in touch with the others and Peter," she half-jokingly said it but Liz knew she meant it.

She just decided to keep quiet but she had vented her feelings that was a start she knew deep down that Max could not exist without her sister, Rose and Peter and was so sad.

Liz knew that she was feeling hemmed in in Scotland, she felt she needed to spread her wings elsewhere, maybe live somewhere else, settle somewhere else on their own without living under the same roof as the others.

"This is what we should be doing with our lives," said Max. "We should be thankful for what we have got and enjoy it. We're millionaires and we need to start behaving like them."

Liz laughed. "It is not until the end of the year Max that's nearly ten months away yes but nothing like planning ahead. It will be a holiday for the two of us and no one else."

Despite Max's promises Liz knew deep down how she would probably behave in the next ten months before the biggest exhibition of all. She knew where her path lay she felt the talk was all for nothing and that Max was probably just saying what she wanted to hear. There was no doubt that Max loved her but sometimes her mind took over.

Rose and Mary were already making plans for the ceremony so the five days they spent with each other consisted of them making time for each other. After all this time together they now knew their relationship needed to be rebuilt on trust and love.

As the days went on they enjoyed each other's company more and took time for each other. Liz was almost taken in by the way Max behaved.

"Rose will be in her element," remarked Liz.

"Yes and Mary will be champing at the bit too, let them plan away while we enjoy each other." Max replied looking lovingly at Liz with so much tenderness.

Liz quite liked the idea of staying a while in Paris she knew Marianne was living there and wondered if Max had any thoughts of sleeping with her again. She would not ask her at the moment. For now they had so much to look forward to they had so much to repair.

They even found time to catch up with Peter and his partner Adam who had flown over from their beautiful home in Italy.

Chapter 13

Peter and Liz had met briefly when they were at college and he never forgot the presence that Liz had whenever she walked into a room. They later met again as his career took off. He was an agent then and was determined to make it as a publicist. He began to look after some celebrities and met up with Liz as she and Sam began to make a name for themselves.

He was largely responsible for their big break and Liz never forgot that. He just seemed to know the right people and would always be in the right place at the right time. As his business began to flourish it was obvious to Liz that he needed a cash injection so that he could promote himself. Liz had always ensured she had her own bank account and after a long conversation with Peter on how he could grow his business she leant him a vast amount of money. She and Sam were in the big league now earning a fortune very quickly. Liz called it a loan and wrote him a cheque.

"I can't accept this," he said to Liz, "it's a fortune."

"It will make you want you want to be," she replied looking straight into his eyes and pressed the cheque into his hand.

"I can't pay you back right away."

"Look," she replied. "Don't worry about that for now we will just call it a loan I have more than enough."

Even at this early stage she was clever with money she would never have given it to him if she thought she could not manage and on paper she and Sam were already millionaires.

Peter was tall with blond hair and blue eyes. He was kind considerate and thoroughly devoted to Liz. They had struck up a friendship that would be tested throughout the years.

He had never once spoken ill of Sam even though he could see through her at times. He knew how much Liz loved her and to break her heart by telling her about the other women would have been so unfair.

He had often suspected she took soft drugs but after everything that had happened in Scotland was surprised when the truth came out about the hard drugs. He would have done anything for Liz and always maintained he would be there for her. This would prove to be so true as the time went on.

He had journeyed through adulthood with one or two boyfriends but no one special. Then he met Adam. Adam had been a driver for the celebrities and was working hard in his own company as driver for the stars. Liz and Sam had put on a huge charity ball and Adam was driving that night as one of his staff was off sick.

Peter was immediately attracted to him as Liz introduced them to each other. They never spent another night apart. As their business's flourished Peter became a well know publicist and Adam now owned a private plane which was now used instead of cars. They had it all and had been together for ever as Liz would often remark. Peter often thought that if Liz and Sam ever split up he would find her the perfect partner as she had for him.

Chapter 14

One evening Peter and Liz were alone together as the other two were out. Adam had offered to drive Max to a small exhibition she wanted to see. At one time Liz would have gone with her – Max would have insisted but now things were different. Peter noticed immediately that maybe things were not as they should be between them.

Peter looked at Liz deep in her eyes.

"Is this what you really want Liz? You seem so distant these days. Are you ready for a ceremony, the commitment? I know things are not right between you two. Can I help?"

"Peter," she sighed her eyes sad. "I feel I'm on an express train. I've tried to talk to Max but you know what she's like and the others will be planning ahead I feel I can't get off this rollercoaster."

He saw the look in her eyes and for the first time since they had been together was concerned.

"But you love each other so much Liz it would seem to be a natural progression in your relationship. What's wrong I thought everything was fine between you."

"Maybe we just want different things now in our lives," she said gently.

This was now turning into a very deep conversation and Liz was beginning to feel uncomfortable. She felt she owed a debt to Max. She had to now persuade Peter everything was ok. She dare not tell him how frightened she was of her when her temper was bubbling.

"Of course I love her and yes it's what I want."

He looked again at her

"You've almost persuaded me Liz." He put on a false smile, she knew he knew all was not well.

"Actually Adam and I are tying the knot later this year but it will be very low key, yours of course will be a big circus you do realise that," and laughed again nervously.

He then looked at her and held both her hands.

"Whatever the future holds Liz I will always be there for you wherever you are I am always a phone call away."

He had a terrible sense of foreboding but did not know why and dare not tell her. Liz was his greatest friend apart from Adam. He adored her and would always protect her as best he could. It was as if she was his little sister.

Max and Adam returned and they spent the rest of the evening wining and dining. Peter knew Max was heading for the greatest moment of her life when the Paris exhibition opened. She would be the global success and he just hoped her mental state would not interfere with her and Liz's relationship any more than it had done already

They said their goodbyes and Liz was sad when she saw them leave. He was without doubt one of her greatest friends. He knew her inside out. Was she going through with the ceremony for her or for Max? She now began to wonder.

She was thinking of a lot of things now about her life and relationship. She thought of Susan at the stables and how she suddenly longed to be with her – was that so wrong?

They eventually returned home determined to ensure that the four of them would not be in each other's pockets so much.

"I've made dinner for us tonight so we'll see you at seven. Great to see you back we can go over all the plans tonight," said Mary and she was gone.

They didn't have a chance to say no. Max and Liz looked at each other and sighed. Within minutes their new found freedom and independence had disappeared. Dutifully they went next door that evening and although they wanted to be on their own it turned into a very nice pleasant almost like a bonding time.

Rose seemed on top form again and very bright almost wide eyed. Liz noticed how on the go she appeared but did not think any more of it. The drink flowed very freely and Rose seemed to be on top of the world with all of her organising and notes reams of notes for everything as usual.

Liz and Max eventually got into bed in the early hours too tired even to make love. Liz was almost thankful that Max was too tired or too drunk. The evening had worn Liz out – all the talking had made it hard for her to concentrate and Rose had been like an unexploded bomb with all of her plans.

Nothing had changed she thought as she fell asleep but not in Max's arms. She rarely slept in her arms anymore Max had begun to frighten her with her strength and moods.

Max woke and looked at her as she slept. She was concerned about the behaviour of Rose the night before and thought she would talk to her later that morning. Liz was utterly exhausted and her face showed it as she slept, it also showed a look of worry and concern which she had never noticed before.

No gym for you tomorrow she thought. She needed to show Liz how she could change and be the Max she once was. She needn't have worried Liz didn't stir until nine. Max had rung Michael and explained she would not be working out once again organising Liz.

"No worries," he replied. It was unlike Liz not to train and he and Sarah made a mental note of it in case it began to form a pattern.

"Maybe we could meet up later tonight I know Liz has missed you guys." It would be a nice surprise for her. She was trying to make an effort and include Liz more and be more thoughtful.

"Sure," and they made arrangements where to meet.

The evening was just what Liz and Max needed. There was no talk of art, ceremonies or even her 40th which was later in the winter. They talked of the charity run that they were organising briefly, but on the whole they just enjoyed the evening toasting the happy couple and generally chatting.

It would mean more training which they hoped she could combine with her usual workout and of course the writing that she was about to embark on. Max showed enthusiasm and support for Liz and Michael and Sarah breathed a sigh of relief. It looked as though everything was going to work out in the end.

Max was often slightly jealous of the friendship Liz had formed with Michael and Sarah. She was never excluded from anything but she just felt as though she was intruding sometimes in their own energetic athlete world.

Max noticed how at ease Liz was with the pair and almost felt a pang of jealousy. They all got on so well and she began to realise how alone Liz must have been feeling. She had entrusted her life with them and they ensured she was looked after at all times. This was something Max should have been doing but she had got too involved with her work.

She should have been able to talk to Liz about their relationship. It was obvious that Michael and Sarah knew that things had not been right between them but they were very discreet and ensured that Max was involved in the whole conversation that night.

Max would have to ensure that she did not show the jealousy and anger that was beginning to form. The evening though was thoroughly enjoyed by them all. They went back to Michael and Sarah's for a night cap and Max again noticed how at home Liz was there.

She had obviously been spending some time there. Max pretended not to show any emotion but deep down knew she would have to pay far more attention to Liz. Liz was still drifting away and was looking as if she could be quite independent these days.

She had to make things right between them and vowed to make more of an effort and be considerate in the bedroom as she knew she was far too demanding and would ensure she was more thoughtful in future.

She also knew that Susan was beginning to play a bigger part in her life. She felt guilty for having met up and slept with Marianne on those occasions which all added tension which did her temper no good. As they got home in the early hours their home was in darkness.

Max was pleased as she knew there would be interruptions. She planned to indulge Liz when they got to bed and continue to try to make things right between them. As far as Max was concerned if things were ok in the bedroom then everything was fine.

As soon as they got in she gently pulled her towards her.

"You know I love you don't you Liz?" as she began to kiss her. "I want to make it right between us like it used to be. You believe me don't you?"

"Of course I do," replied Liz, as she responded to her, beginning to caress her in return, this was what she wanted the gentle thoughtful caring Max. She craved her body and her loving.

"Thank god you're back!" cried Mary.

The lights went on as Mary stood in the lounge area. She had been waiting for them to return. It was just gone midnight and she was determined to talk about the ceremony at this time of night.

"I need to know about these people who you have put on the guest list Liz, I don't know them."

Max stood there furious. Before she could speak it was Liz who took over.

"Not now Mary please." As she began to button up her shirt.

"But I need to know I have so much to do and Rose is far too busy with another project."

"Not now Mary," said Liz more firmly.

She looked at Max turned and went upstairs.

"You sort it out Max." And was gone.

Max was furious.

"Mary this has to stop now. We need this time together you can't keep barging in like this. You're my sister and I love you but Liz and I need to be together things are not as good as they should be, we need this time."

The look on Max's face was enough to tell her that Max was boiling in rage. She was worried as these days Max's fuse was getting shorter and shorter.

She breathed deeply. "Max I'm sorry you are quite right forgive me. I just so want to get it all right for your special day."

She hugged her sister, no response Max was sick and tired of it all and wondered if things would ever change for the better.

Mary left forlorn as Max went to the kitchen and poured herself a large scotch. She was drinking more these days she knew it. The more she drank the less Liz drank.

She gulped the drink and began to calm down then poured herself another one then went upstairs.

Liz was in bed asleep. As she undressed she sat on the edge of the bed and looked out of the window at the loch. She turned and looked at Liz and climbed into bed beside her and held her. She began to caress her and kiss her neck as eventually Liz awoke to her touch. Max wanted her then and now and nothing was going to stop her. Liz was getting used to this sort of behaviour from Max and just accepted what was about to happen.

Max professed undying love as usual as she quite harshly fulfilled Liz. Liz began to respond but Max demanded far more from her and at a much faster pace. Liz cried out as Max almost hurt her as she took her roughly to the point of ecstasy. Liz then afterwards began to kiss Max gently as she explored her body as if to show Max want she wanted but Max grabbed her hand and ensured she entered her quickly as she climaxed.

The time when they spent hours fulfilling each other had sometimes gone nowadays everything was so rushed and Liz did not like it.

Eventually they fell into a deep sleep. For Liz it was another troubled sleep, this was not what she wanted. She wanted the gentleness that Max had once found. Max was now just take take take. She cried silently as the tears slowly rolled down her face lying away from Max. She wondered if she was doing the right thing in agreeing to marry her.

Yes she had not refused Max and had in the end almost enjoyed her but the constant waking her up when it suited was not what she had signed up for all those years ago. She had to talk to Max about it again and soon.

She worried so much nothing was changing she thought. It will always be the same.

Max awoke the next day first. Liz was not there. She thought back to last night and a pang of guilt set in. She had a terrible hangover and realised she had done exactly what she promised she would never do again. She knew Liz would be in the gym she would make it up to her later. She looked for Rose.

Chapter 15

Max made a point of talking to Rose the next day. She had her suspicions about her behaviour but wanted to be sure of things. She played her cards well and began her conversation.

"Rose you seem so busy these days how on earth do you manage to keep going don't you ever sleep?"

Rose looked rather sheepish.

"Of course I sleep I just don't need as much as I used to."

"Rose be honest with me. What's going on?" Max asked almost gently.

Eventually Rose told the truth. "I have been taking these pills they help me to keep going. I have so much to do there just isn't the time."

"What pills Rose? What on earth you are talking about?"

Rose reluctantly showed the bottle. They were prescription only but clearly stated to avoid alcohol.

"How often do you take these Rose, what are they for?"

"They just help me cope with things Max. Don't worry yourself."

Max was worried though as Rose had been drinking last night and at times had seemed like a woman possessed.

"Just promise me you'll be careful you were not yourself last night I'm sure you shouldn't have been drinking and taking them at the same time Rose you could do yourself some damage."

"Max," Rose now looked cross, "I'm fine I know what I'm doing if you think I'm a problem then maybe you should get yourself another secretary, assistant, planner and organiser."

Max was shocked and upset.

"Rose don't be like that it's because I care. I am worried about you we all are."

"Then let's just drop it. They help me keep going when I'm tired and believe me Max you exhaust me when we are planning your exhibitions everything is always on your terms. And as for Liz we all have to keep our eye on her making sure she is ok. It's been five years now have you opened your eyes lately? She's better than she has ever been. Look at her Max – she's distancing herself from us and you don't even notice. She needs to find her own identity we have taken it from her. Look what we have done to her look what she has become," she carried on with her tirade.

"She has recovered as much as she is ever going to Max, let her lead her own life. We always have to pander to her don't we? All the plans and ideas and work I have to do around you I am exhausted. We can't disturb you we have to live under your rules. She has to be cosseted, can't you see you are driving her away? Maybe she is too far away already does she really deep down want to marry you or is she doing it to please you?"

The words stung Max and hurt her deeply. No one had spoken to her like this for years. Max responded bitterly.

"Well maybe you are spending too much time in our house we all need the space. She has agreed to marry me she wouldn't have said yes if she did not want to."

Rose backed down and quietly this time replied.

"Is it what she wants or what you want Max? I've seen how sad she is sometimes while she is here her eyes light up when she is going to the village."

She would think later to what Rose had said. This was certainly not like Rose but Max backed down. She went over and hugged Rose trying to make the situation better.

"I'm sorry Rose, please is there anything I can do? Let's not fall out perhaps we all need to sit down and sort out some ground rules again."

Rose calmed down. "Yes maybe you are right I'm sorry too I've just got a lot of things to do I'll be fine."

Max would have cause to remember her words later on. Max knew that writing the book would ensure Liz did not stay in the gym too long. While Liz was having some of the tests done she had chatted to the doctor explaining what was going on in their lives. This will do her good it will be something else to focus on.

Chapter 16

It had been decided by all of them that Liz's book would be written at home. The problem was Liz needed somewhere quiet to work. Rose and Mary had a large part of the 'library area' for their work. It had been furnished with expensive computers and other equipment. Every night Rose as ever would tidy up and put things back where they were supposed to be. In the morning very often papers would be strewn everywhere as Liz or Max had been looking for something.

They were the most untidy couple she knew yet she would not have it any other way. A decision had to made as to where would Liz work with Jaime who was going to help bring her diary to life.

While Liz had been in hospital recovering from the attack and later the clinic Max would bring the plan of the two homes to show her. It was Liz who had wanted the whole of the loft converted into their private area. Max had already occupied some of the loft for her studio. Liz wanted their bedroom and bathroom up there.

There was even enough space for a room that would become their dayroom. The views were spectacular across Loch Ness from the loft area. Liz just did not want to sleep at ground level but never explained why. So the large room which should have been the bedroom had really been dormant for the past four years.

"Perfect," said Liz, "we'll use that room."

Excitedly she had it decorated and furnished it to her taste plenty of natural wood and stone. Max was so pleased she was not going to travel daily to write the book.

"After all I do not see how you would have had the time to travel every day we need to make things right between us and maybe we could make some special time for each other like we used to." Max was trying hard to build on their relationship.

In the beginning after the 'accident' Liz spent three structured and planned hours in the gym every day followed by a swim. It was this religious training that kept her in such great shape. She would push herself to the point of exhaustion but she loved it. She would then spend time with Max and they would talk about the day. Those days had fast disappeared as Liz was now training for marathons their lives were so different nowadays

Lunch had usually been with the other two and then the afternoons were spent with Liz doing her own thing walking, visiting the business in the village. Now Liz was hardly at the house during the day and the other three were always busy. Max's work ensured she was always busy becoming under more and more pressure.

The day had arrived for the writer – Jaime to arrive. All four of them waited in apprehension. At the allotted time of two pm she arrived to be welcomed by Liz and Max. As the other two were introduced Max noticed Mary's eyes light up.

She looked across and saw the disappointment in Rose's eyes but thought nothing of it. Rose and Mary left after an hour or so ensuring Max and Liz could settle Jaime in and make some plans.

"Come on Mary let's just go home for the rest of the day we are finished here."

They took the corridor back home and Rose ensured they shut the door behind them firmly to prevent Mary from interfering as she tended to do so much nowadays.

It was decided that they would write for a couple of hours in the afternoons. Jaime had a fair journey and it was Max who suggested that if things looked like they were going on later into the evening then she should stay.

At first Jaime commuted – the drive was about an hour each way but eventually she stayed over as she felt a tension building in the houses and she wanted to get her work done with Liz as quickly as she could. She noticed how moody Max could be and she began to see another side to the flamboyant artist.

"I don't think I will be here for much longer Max," she announced one day. "I have worked already on the book I just need some input from you all it should only take about a couple of months for the first draft."

There were still two spare bedrooms – huge, on the ground floors which were rarely used except when Peter came and stayed so space was not a problem.

Liz wanted Max to be part of the writing experience and very often they would go up to the studio to get some ideas and memories from her but she had to pick her moments.

As the weeks went by the book was going very well and Jaime thought it would only take a few more weeks to get the first manuscript off to the editors. Liz still worked out every day which left her on her own for the morning. She managed to get a lot of work done at this time and she fitted in perfectly with the others. She was a very gentle human being with a marvellous sense of humour. Mary especially took to her and soon they became very at ease with each other. Jaime found everything quite daunting to start with but Mary seemed to ensure that she soon became relaxed.

Max spoke to Liz about her concerns with Mary and Rose one night as they lay watching the water on the Loch for once there was no tension between them. Max was making such an effort to win Liz's affection back.

"I've been watching Mary while she's around Jaime. She's like a child in a sweet shop and I don't like it. That is not my sister I don't know what has got into her."

Max felt Liz's body shudder as she spoke. Liz was shocked she had not seen it herself and shaken that her dearest closest friend Rose might be in trouble.

"I thought everything was ok with them now they have been together longer than we have they just go so well together." She was now so upset.

She looked into Max's eyes and saw the concern in them. Max was worried for Rose. They had become very close friends and if her sister was thinking of cheating on her it would be the ultimate betrayal for Rose. Liz by now was wide awake and they sat there talking about what may or may not happen. They seemed to have overcome their differences for the time being but if Mary and Rose cheated on each other she did not think they would recover.

"I didn't even think about Jaime and Mary are you sure?"

As Max explained she just felt things were not right between Mary and Rose and this could just be the diversion that could tip the balance.

"That means we are all in trouble with our relationships then doesn't it?" Liz replied sadly, looking into Max's eyes. "I will talk to Jaime tomorrow first thing."

Liz did speak to her the next day calmly and gently.

"Liz please do not worry about it, I am not interested in women. To be honest I am not looking for another relationship. I had a bad experience years ago with my ex-husband – my life is my writing now. Please Liz do not concern yourself there is nothing for you to worry about."

She had begun to get upset and so Liz did not push it any further. Jaime was a lovely lady but not once did Liz think there was a problem. Then in Liz's world there were never any dark sides, not until now at least.

She decided to talk with Rose and they went out for a walk. Rose hadn't been herself lately. She seemed distant as if she was worried about something. Liz needed to spend some time with her something she hadn't done lately. In fact she realised she hadn't spent quality time with any of them recently.

"I'm just worried about this year there is so much is going on," Rose replied when asked.

Rose wondered if Max had said anything to her about the pills.

They talked for ages openly about everything and nothing. Their friendship was deep and they kept nothing from each other at least Liz didn't. Liz eventually explained how things were not quite the same between her and Max. Rose could see in her eyes how sad she was but knew that Max was making a huge effort to repair the damage already done. Liz didn't mention Susan. That was something she did not want to share, although she felt Rose already knew.

Rose didn't tell her about her real worry. Much much later she realised that she had made a huge mistake in not telling Liz the truth.

Chapter 17

Liz wanted all of her special memories to be absolutely perfect and truthful from her diary so the book had to tell it like it really was. As the writing began Liz began to remember...

A very important part of her recovery had been the beginning of the physical side to the relationship with her and Max and she began to reflect on it. When leaving the clinic and during her therapy it became very apparent that this was a concern for them both. There was no denying the deep love they had for each other, that was unconditional without doubt. Liz however just had no feelings for that part of their relationship. Max although very disappointed to start with, after talking to the medical staff and getting advice realised that they would have to be patient.

The pair talked for hours about the situation and it was agreed that the time would be right when Liz was ready. Max threw herself into her work but never altered the way she was with Liz. She knew deep inside it was a problem for Liz and she did not want to make things seem awkward. Ever since Liz had returned home she had always slept in a vest top and shorts. Max so as not to appear to be pressurising slept in the same attire. She knew Liz was so self-conscious about her scars but in time hopefully this would go.

Liz threw herself into the gym as soon as she was able. It proved to be something of light relief sometimes to be able to relax with other people. Occasionally Max would go down to the gym and watch Liz as she was put through a very hard programme.

Sometimes she would join her at the end for the long swim as gradually Liz became slightly more confident about her body. She had been home for almost four months. It was one morning when Liz went to the fridge that it became apparent to Mary and Rose just how much work Liz was putting in at the gym.

Her body had begun to transform. She was becoming tight, taut, and muscular with most of the fat stripped away. Max realised just how excitable she was looking and gave a whistle. At first she thought she had gone too far especially the way things were physically between them but thankfully the old Liz was returning and she turned round, gave a pose and grinned.

It was a start and as Liz went to work out Max chatted to Rose quietly. Rose knew the how things were and knew how disheartened Max was.

"Just be patient she is as upset as you but everything will work out trust me." She tried to encourage Max.

Max and Rose had become very close friends over the past months and she could see why Liz entrusted herself in Rose. Mary just tended to keep out of those sorts of conversations as even now after everything it was in her eyes Liz who was taking her sister away from her.

Liz woke one morning and Max had one arm across her as if to protect her from everything and as usual was watching her.

"Hello you," said Max. Liz looked at her and smiled.

She had the most unbearable ache in the pit of her stomach, an ache full of longing and love and almost automatically she began to hold Max and begin to caress her.

The look in her eyes was enough for both of them to realise that the physical side of their relationship was about to be rekindled. They held each other tightly knowing they were about to travel down a path they hadn't been for nearly a year and a half.

Max gently kissed Liz who responded passionately. Their hands gently and carefully began to explore their bodies as the tension between them began to grow. They began to whisper things to each other as their passion began to build.

They were suddenly interrupted by Mary who stood there in their bedroom; how long she had been there they did not know.

"There you are I was wondering if everything was ok. You hadn't come down and Michael is here Liz, and oh... I'm sorry if I oh I'll see you her later," and quickly disappeared back down the stairs

Liz didn't say a word Max was outraged but was silent.

"Come on," said Liz, "I need to get to work and so do you." As she kissed her on the mouth gently.

The moment was lost but at least there had been a moment.

Liz worked out in an infuriating pace. She still had the aching feeling and she knew today would be the day when she and Max would be together again. Max went to the kitchen area still angry, for once she noticed how comfortable the other two were in their home. They were sitting at the table eating breakfast reading the papers discussing the day – but in Max and Liz's home. She was now beginning to realise why Liz had wanted all their private rooms in the loft space.

Even while so desperately ill she had the foresight to try to prevent what had just happened. It was she, Max, who had allowed this to happen and now it needed to stop. The bubble was beginning to burst. Maybe just she and Liz should be on their own at breakfast and not all four of them. She would certainly ponder this thought over the next few days.

"I'm sorry Max, I didn't mean to startle or interrupt anything. I just worried when you hadn't come down for breakfast this morning."

"Forget it," she replied.

Max looked at Rose with a stare that spelt volumes. Rose knew what had been interrupted. Max began to get some champagne from the fridge.

"Bit early for that isn't it?" said Mary.

Max took a deep breath as she searched for an ice bucket. Rose as ever the diplomat suggested that she and Mary go to Inverness for a long lunch. Mary began to protest saying she had too much work to do. Max looked as though she would explode.

"No," said Rose firmly, "we are going out for the day. My treat."

Mary still protested but eventually gave up as Rose had decided that all work would stop for the day, emails could be answered later. Anyway they had pc and office equipment in their house which they could use later on. Maybe the office could move next door thought Max. Maybe they could have their home back. She would try to get everything on track for Liz.

Max then went to what they called the day room. Like the rest of their home it was full of beams and wood. She arranged the day bed with furs and cushions and then placed rose petals over them. She ensured candles were ready to be lit as she looked at the time. Liz would be finished in about an hour.

This gave her enough time to have a nice shower and dress. She knew where the day was going and so ensured everything was just right for Liz. She wanted to everything to be perfect especially today.

She chose a linen shirt with buttons that were easy to unfasten. She smiled, she had thought of everything. Liz sometimes had difficulty in the simplest of tasks and the last thing she wanted was for her to feel uncomfortable. She wanted everything to be as near perfect as could be.

As Liz was late for her training session she didn't finish until one in the afternoon. Michael and Sarah were fine about the late start. The three of them had formed a strong friendship and she was able to talk to them about everything.

She trusted them completely, a trust that would prove to be invaluable eventually. She finished a pounding swim as Michael watched over her.

"You are looking so good these days you can see the work you have put in. You look like an athlete ready for the Olympics." He laughed.

Liz had spoken to them both about earlier in the day. His towering frame blocked out the winter sun.

"Jeez you look so hot right now, go to her and enjoy her."

Sarah agreed. "Go on Liz enjoy the day, the time is right for you get your life back."

She knew she looked hot and she felt ready to take the next step with Max. She kissed them on the cheek and high fived as usual,

"See you tomorrow."

"Ah ah, day off tomorrow, you are going to need it now go and enjoy and relax."

And then they were off.

She showered and put on her 'uniform' clean vest top and baggy long shorts. She looked at herself in the mirror and liked what she saw. She made her way to the kitchen area and looked across to where Rose and Mary were usually hard at work. Silence.

She grabbed a bottle of champagne noticing that one was missing and smiled to herself. It was as if she knew Max had already taken one up. She went upstairs to the studio where Max was sitting working on a painting.

"Hi," she said quietly as she stood behind her looking at the work.

Max had been having a problem with a particular piece and she noticed now that she had overcome it. She placed her chin on her shoulder standing behind her as she never failed to marvel at the brilliance of her work.

"You smell nice," she whispered as she gently moved her still damp hair and kissed her neck.

She knew Max was wearing nothing under the shirt. Max closed her eyes as Liz slowly twirled the swivel chair round and looked into her eyes. The ache inside her was almost too much to bear as she kissed her at first gently.

Max immediately responded and began to hold her. Their mouths and tongues explored each other as again like earlier their passion began to grow.

Liz then slowly undid the shirt that Max had decided to wear. Liz had forgotten the softness and the beauty of another woman's body as she began to kiss and caress it.

"Let's go somewhere more comfortable," as Max took Liz by the hand.

Their dayroom was filled with lit candles and the perfume from the rose petals was perfect. Liz allowed Max help her take off her clothes for the first time since her return as Max held her gently caressing and kissing her. She was careful not to let Liz feel uncomfortable as they continued to undress each other.

Liz kissed Max longingly as she began to caress her body kissing her everywhere. She gently kissed her breasts brushing them with the back of her hand sending small shivers down Max's back. Her hand and mouth gently moved over her body teasing and tantalising her until they made their way between her thighs. As her hand moved slowly further up she knew Max was ready for her as began to take Max to a point of no return again and again. Max held her tightly as she climaxed again and again. Max's cries of delight would definitely have been heard if Rose and Mary had been downstairs.

At one point there were tears of joy and Max even thought she may have passed out for a split second as Liz continued to fulfil her. Eventually it was Max who then began to pleasure Liz. She was so gentle at first as Liz said huskily

"I won't break."

A whole host of emotions were released by Liz as her whole body became alive again to the touch of Max. She was so gentle with her tantalising her, teasing her, kissing every part of her body.

Her hand and mouth followed a trail down her body as she kissed her scars that had bothered Liz so much ensuring that she did not feel they were unsightly or embarrassing. She kissed her back where the knife had hurt her and opened her up so brutally.

Finally her hand moved to her thigh as she kissed her legs and as she entered her Liz gasped as again and again she too climaxed repeatedly. She held onto Max as tears flowed from her eyes, she adored her so much and now they were back together again.

Much much later Max woke and realised for the first time they had fallen into a deep sleep totally entwined with each other. She looked at Liz's body, still very scarred and raw from the attack and the many operations she had endured. She marvelled at the way Liz had worked so hard to bring her body to the peak condition it was in.

Liz woke as Max began to kiss her scars gingerly and carefully so as not to upset her. It was her way of ensuring Liz that they did not worry or repulse her. Again they both responded to each other this time harder and faster until they could take no more. It was almost as if they had been together for the first time like all those years ago.

"We need champagne," said Max as she kissed her on the mouth.

Liz looked at her and said very quietly that at least this time Mary would not be bursting through the door like she did that first time. They both laughed but knew deep down that Mary was becoming something of an annoyance...

"Hey is this what writers do in the day?" said Max, as she walked in to the bathroom.

Liz was remembering the first time since she came home that their physical side of the relationship was cemented. Max had driven into Inverness to finalise another exhibition leaving Liz working on the book. She bent down and kissed Liz who held her hand out inviting her to join her.

Her eyes said join me.

As she held her hand out to Max. "I was remembering the first time you and I got together when I returned from the hospital."

Max climbed into the bath and sat behind Liz cradling her and kissing her back for once being gentle and caring.

They talked for ages as they looked out over the Loch. Liz wanted Max to remember so much and would constantly ask questions, she wanted to ensure that everything was just right. This was why they should be not rushing round all over the world constantly, thought Liz.

There were no doors upstairs just the flight of stone stairs. Often Rose might begin to climb them and then realise that they weren't to be disturbed. It was proving to be a problem now after all this time with Mary. Liz never complained but inside she was becoming a bit agitated. Max knew there was a predicament forming and could see this could escalate if they were not careful.

"I'll Speak to Rose and see what she thinks we should do," said Max. She never did.

Not one day went without Rose thinking about the past and how now, after all these years she had not told the truth. It tortured her terribly but it was too late to talk about it now – or so she thought.

Rose had opened the post as usual. They had so much post to handle that it took her and Mary a couple of hours each day to attend to it. One letter hand written caught Rose's eye and she immediately hid it. She would open it later. It was addressed to her but she sensed it would prove to be dreadful. She went for a walk later and opened the letter privately.

It was from Emma the woman who had been at the beginning of all the trouble with Sam. Sam had been released from hospital and Emma had intimated she would be getting in touch about some cinema tickets again.

Rose understood the cryptic message and tried to work out what to do. What had happened between Liz herself and indeed Sam was years ago, Liz had never remembered it so in fact had never lied to Max. Rose had assured them all that nothing had happened but she had lied. The truth would hurt them all but she was beginning to feel cornered. She knew she need to tell Mary about the letter but the timing just wasn't right.

She would have to talk to Mary about it and confess her shameful past and soon. She thought afterwards she should have told Mary when the other two were away. That way she would have had Mary's complete attention.

Chapter 18

Liz and Max returned from their break both excited about their forthcoming ceremony. It would be a quiet affair no paparazzi no crowds just the people from the estate... That is how Liz and Max wanted it.

Word had got out about the ceremony and there were calls from magazines offering huge amounts of money to cover the story. It was now that Max and Liz realised how well known they had become. They received more and more mail from well wishers and fans.

Liz knew she would not have a say in the preparations for the service so took a back seat on all the arrangements. Mary and Rose worked out the best dates and announced matter of factly over dinner one evening that it was to be held in a few weeks. Plans were put into motion and the castle was booked.

Liz and Max had no say in the matter Mary in her masterful way was allowed to organise everything. The service and reception was held in a huge castle overlooking a loch and the close friends they had were given rooms and suites for the night.

Up until the day Peter was concerned for Liz but during the service he was almost taken in by the way Liz was. She loved Max and Max loved her they just had to work out the problems they had had.

Both women exchanged wonderful words to each other and there was not a dry eye in the building as they sealed their love with rings. It was a marvellous time for them both and Liz reflected later on the wonderful arrangements that Mary and Rose had made. Nothing was forgotten and every guest was treated beautifully.

Liz had to hand it to Mary she had outdone all her expectations. The day was perfect. Liz thoroughly enjoyed herself and ensured that every person invited was spoken to at length and thanked for everything they had every done for her. She was so happy and didn't want the day to end.

Max and Liz looked wonderful and their guests were treated to such luxury. Everyone from the estate was invited and the day and evening was one of the most magical they had ever been to.

The newspapers covered the story and a national well-known magazine was given permission to photograph the whole event. All the money paid to them from the magazines was donated and went to the hospital where Liz had been recovering for so long. Liz looked at Max lovingly as she suggested it. This was how it should be the two of them back together mentally and physically.

As the day progressed speeches were made and Max was marvellous as she spoke so lovingly about Liz. Mary and Rose also made wonderful speeches about the couple and everyone there was in full spirits as the day turned into the evening. There was plenty of singing and dancing just like at the huge party that Liz had organised earlier in the year.

Max began to get drunk as the evening went on but for once she was the happy drunk. Liz enjoyed herself and watched as the other three became more and more intoxicated as the night wore on. There were no bad feelings from anyone and the singing and dancing carried on until the early hours when finally the happy couple decided that the party had to end.

For Liz it was a happy day but on reflection much later she realised it was not the happiest. Peter noticed as she watched Max and the other two as they drank their way through the reception. He looked at Liz his heart sad. She had gone through this day for Max he knew that. His beloved Liz, he just hoped she would not come to any harm. He remembered what Rose had sometimes remarked on that Max could change at a drop of a hat when drinking too much and he prayed she would not hurt Liz.

The reception was the talk of the whole area for a long time. Everyone had been made to feel special that day and it was all down to the wonderful heart that Liz possessed. While the other three enjoyed themselves and devoured alcohol Liz ensured everyone present was looked after implicitly.

The photos did everyone justice and it was decided that Liz could choose which ones were to be published. They gave the impression of the fairytale that they once were living. No one would have guessed what was really going on in their lives. No one except a few close friends of Liz. These people were just thankful that the day had gone off without a hitch.

As the guests left in mini buses to go home there was just a handful of very close friends staying at the castle. Once it all became quiet Peter noticed how distant Liz immediately became. Max and the other three were still drinking and laughing and joking but Liz did not seem to be included. She wandered around the function room and he watched her as she sat quietly looking out over the loch. He went over to her with some brandies.

"Come on have this, a perfect ending to a perfect day," he said quietly. This was not the time to talk about his thoughts.

She smiled looking exhausted, she had managed to keep up the appearance of happiness all day and now just a little of her guard was dropping. They sat together and Adam joined them as they waited for the others.

About half an hour later Max noticed Liz was missing and came and found her with the others. She went over to her putting on a huge show of tenderness.

"Come on," she said. "Let's go to bed."

Liz was so tired and was thankful they were going to their suite. She dreaded what would happen next but she needn't have worried. Max was the most considerate and gentle she could have been for once and passionately and lovingly ensured that Liz enjoyed her wedding night. Perhaps the other two had had words before. Liz was relieved that Max hadn't been her usual forceful self and afterwards slept well. She treated her so tenderly and gently kissing her telling her how much she loved her, how she was the happiest woman in the world. The next morning very much later they woke together and Liz hoped that last night would be a fresh start for them. They lay entwined and Liz just thought about the day before and hoped so much that things would now work out. Max woke and immediately looked into her eyes and hugged her tightly.

She had a dreadful hangover and Liz knew it. They remained still together and Liz drifted off to sleep again. It was almost lunchtime when they woke again this time both feeling much better.

The rest of the day was spent quietly and happily with the others they walked and swam and had a wonderful day. The evening was a quiet affair with the eight of them having a meal. The next day they returned home as they had decided their honeymoon would after all be in Paris after the exhibition it was what Max wanted.

The next few weeks were taken at a slower pace with Max trying her best to assure Liz that everything was ok. She was kind gentle and Liz was thrilled things were going in the right direction.

About a month after the ceremony Liz had received a letter from her solicitor giving an update on Sam. Sam had been released from hospital and had then been in another form of institution for a year. Several months ago she had returned home to her parents. She had made a full recovery, was clean from drugs and was a reformed character and was not a threat to anyone but she would not be coming to Scotland.

Liz's face lost the entire colour as the other three looked on in horror. Her body shuddered and it looked as though she might faint.

"Whatever is it?" Max asked immediately concerned.

Rose already knew what was wrong. The look of fear and terror in Liz's eyes was enough to tell her, her biggest nightmare was about to come true.

Liz was shaking from head to toe as Max held her tightly. Mary and Rose looked on in shock as Max took the letter and read it to them. It was Mary who seemed to take over the situation.

"Let's ring the solicitor and see what we can do?"

"No, look read it," said Max furiously. "It says she is no danger I will never let her near Liz you will be safe my darling," and held Liz tightly.

Rose was ashen and silent, which Max noticed but thought nothing of it. Mary was not convinced and the next few hours were spent with phone calls to various people and eventually she was assured that there was nothing to worry about, Sam had a form of curfew and there was no likelihood of her getting to Scotland again. She was living quietly studying and being well looked after she was not a threat. Mary relented eventually, she was determined that nothing would ruin her sister's career.

Liz had gone for a long run in the afternoon to think about everything. There was nothing else she could do. Max eventually found her later in the afternoon at a place where Liz used to sit and just watch the loch. It was so quiet and peaceful there. She said nothing just held Liz gently suddenly Liz felt so small and lifeless.

"It will be ok you will never see her again I will see to that. No one will ever hurt you again," these words would haunt her for ever.

In the space of a few hours Liz had taken so many steps backwards and they all needed to repair the damage quickly – she was now very vulnerable. They talked for a while and then slowly went back home. Rose met them her eyes so full of worry.

Liz and Max were more and more concerned about Rose. She seemed so preoccupied and looked dreadful. Mary was also very worried and confided in her sister that something was wrong.

"She just won't talk to me she just clams up I don't know what to do." Mary was so upset.

Max took Rose out for a drive to try to talk to her. Rose was getting in deeper and deeper with worry. She knew that the truth would come out and that all four of them stood to be damaged by it.

She explained to Max that a long time ago something had happened through no real fault of her own and now it had come back to rise to the surface. She didn't elaborate or tell her everything, Max listened and her heart went out to her. She couldn't believe that Rose had ever broken the speed limit and yet she was so upset by it all. Rose knew she needed to speak to Mary and soon.

The CD was of course sent to Rose. She knew what it was immediately. She started to sob uncontrollably as Mary looked on in horror.

"Whatever is it Rose talk to me please what is it?"

The time had come for the truth. Rose then began to tell Mary everything. After all this time she now at last was unveiling what had happened. Mary looked at her shocked as the truth was unravelled by Rose. Eventually they called Max in. Somehow Rose found the strength and over the next few hours explained everything.

Mary at last had proved what she thought had happened all along. It was almost a sense of relief for her to know that all her suspicions had been proved right. Rose and Liz had slept together. Rose had lied to them both for all these years.

Max looked on in horror as Rose somehow got the words out. Liz wasn't to blame she knew nothing about it the next day. The three then spent the next few days deciding what to do. All in all it was about a week before they decided when they would sit down to talk to Liz.

Max now had to take on board everything she had been told. Her beloved Liz. Her perfect Liz. She had trouble accepting what had happened and begun to drink even more. They vowed not to say anything to Liz. She had the book to complete. Max was working so hard the timing was all wrong.

Liz was at the stables she still visited there one or two days a week after training for an hour or so before the writing began. Liz and Susan had made a mistake but now things were back to how they should be.

They had talked about it and got over it. Liz valued her job more and she knew Max knew what had happened. Sometimes they talked about what might have been but there was not the tension between them now. They both knew if something went wrong with Max and Liz it might be a different story.

It was to prove to be the biggest mistake that Max had made in her life. They should have told Liz there and then but she had chosen to stay with the others on this. It was Mary and Rose who decided that they would wait until Liz had completed the book. They would have to wait a few more weeks, Max was desolate. The book had to be finished they had to get the book out of the way before they told her.

She found it difficult to look at Liz her wife of just over a couple of months during this time. The honeymoon period seemed to be over. The relationship was beginning to suffer again and now Liz wondered whether she had made a huge mistake.

Mary had insisted they signed a pre-nuptial agreement. Liz had not wanted to but in hindsight she was beginning to think it had been a good idea. Max however now as the days drew on began to feel a rage and jealousy form. On a bad day when things were frantic she was too upset to even look at Liz. She took to painting through the night again it kept her away from Liz she was scared of her own strength, her temper.

She had very roughly taken Liz on several occasions leaving bite marks again which she naturally apologised profusely for the next day. Michael and Sarah were becoming worried again. Liz was spending more time at the stables as the book just needed a few loose ends tightening up and riding more with Susan. They were beginning to talk about her marriage as Susan noticed the marks.

"It's not right Liz why do you let her do this to you?"

As they went back to the stables she could see how sad Liz was.

"Come on have a coffee with me," and Liz went to her apartment.

Sarah saw them go in and knew things were coming to a head in everyone's relationships.

Susan and Liz talked for hours Liz was so sad. No one made a move they just talked and talked as Liz began to cry. Susan gently put her arm round her as she sobbed. She didn't know what to say to her, she just knew she wanted her there and then.

Eventually Liz looked up at her and Susan kissed her lightly on the mouth. Liz wanted her and they made their way to the bedroom. She knew it was wrong they both did. Liz was not in the right frame of mind to have sex with anyone let alone someone other than Max.

Yet make love they did. They could not keep their hands off each other as they realised that maybe this was the right thing to do for them at that time at that place in their lives. There was no regret from them afterwards they just knew for that moment in time they felt as though they were the only people in the world with no other worries. Liz did not love Susan in fact she didn't even know whether she still loved Max anymore. She did not know what she wanted anymore. She just knew she had wanted Susan as much as she had wanted her at that time.

Chapter 19

Liz and Jaime had been working very hard on the book and at last it was finished. Liz and Jaime tidied up things and then Jaime left to compile everything. Liz was relieved it was finished as tensions were becoming rather high in the two households but she did not know why.

Liz was thrilled and relieved it was finished and decided that she and Max would celebrate that evening with some fine wine and food just the two of them. They had not been together physically for a couple of weeks and it troubled Liz. Perhaps a nice meal and some together time would make everything fall back into place. She had cheated on Max but she did not hate herself. Max had treated her shoddily recently but she was prepared to make an effort and support Max at this special time in her life and vowed not to go to the stables for a while. Max always seemed to be preoccupied and appeared to be in another world and was painting furiously as they prepared for the Paris exhibition.

Mary had suggested a meal tentatively, everything seemed so on edge. Liz refused and said that she was cooking a special meal for the two of them that night. She didn't notice the worried look on the others faces.

They chatted quite happily she remembered long afterwards – nothing seemed wrong. They talked about the book and how Max's painting was coming on as she had the exhibition in Paris in the few months. They were discussing travel arrangements nothing seemed untoward.

Deep down Max was beginning to lose control of her temper and a rage was brewing deep down as she drank more and more wine.

Liz was disappointed in the amount she was drinking as she would be taking a bottle of champagne to the bedroom. She had planned the evening and night and wanted Max to remember everything the next day. She began to notice how she was visibly getting more intense as the evening went on.

"What's wrong Max you seem so tense so wound up?"

Max lied. "I'm fine just got a lot to do before tomorrow. I need to send some emails. I know you want tonight to be special Liz so do I," she lied, "but I need to get this done."

Eventually Liz suggested she went up to bed preparing the room with candles and perfume. She wanted everything to be perfect. She wanted Max to be relaxed and not wound up as she had been lately. Liz herself was beginning to relax now that the book was finished, perhaps they could start again and be as they were.

"Don't be too long," she whispered to Max as she kissed the back of her neck. "I want you so much," as Max frantically sent emails about the exhibition.

Unusually Max did not look up at her.

"I'll be up as soon as I can but Liz I need to get this organised."

"I thought Rose and Mary and Peter were tending to all the arrangements why are you doing it isn't that why we pay them?" The word flew from her mouth but Max didn't even seem to notice.

"Liz," now she looked up her eyes beginning to look angry. "Please just let me get this sorted I'll be up shortly."

She knew she was on the edge of exploding but she somehow managed to keep a lid on it. She softened her voice which seemed to reassure Liz.

"Look just make sure the champagne is chilled I'll be up soon. You know how this is. This is the most important exhibition of my life and it has to be right this will make me what I have always dreamed of. Please I won't be long."

In all honesty the last thing she wanted was to be with Liz. She could not get her head around what had been going on with Rose and the past, the lies, the cheating and above all the betrayal. She was boiling into a rage a rage that would prove to be unstoppable. Somehow she managed to persuade Liz to go upstairs.

"I'll be there soon don't worry," she said as calmly as she could it was such a strain and effort to stay calm in front of Liz.

That seemed to work and Liz went up. Max was boiling with rage – the rage that had not shown itself for many many years – she had controlled her temper all these years but now it was too difficult. She was tired, so very tired and getting drunker by the minute then suddenly she remembered the pills that Rose often took just to keep her awake and on top of things. She had drunk too much already.

She rummaged around in Rose's desk found them and simply took a handful without reading the dosage. After all she thought they can't do any harm then took a large swig of whisky as she began at last to watch the CD that had caused all this problem and worry for the three of them. She had not seen it for herself yet and she chose now of all times to watch it – another mistake.

Now with the new found confidence of the pills and the drink she sat down to watch it and was soon appalled at what she saw. In her eyes Liz had lied to her as the bottle of whisky got emptier and emptier.

Liz so wanted to be with Max and she longed for her. It was a couple of hours later when Max staggering came up to bed noisily up the stairs. Liz had fallen asleep, stirred and then woke as she turned and watched Max as she came into the bedroom. She took the bottle of champagne from the ice bucket and took a swig her eyes were wild as she bent down and then started to kiss Liz hard and painfully on the mouth.

"Hey slow down we have plenty of time," she said, concerned she knew she was in for another session according to Max's rules.

She sat up and got out of bed to help Max as she staggered around the room.

"No Max not like this, please not again," she begged her.

Max was past the point of no return and went to grab her viscously. Liz tried to escape the clutches of her as she came towards her again.

As she lunged for her again pushing her hard against the stone wall, her head hit the wall with a thud stunning her. There was no stopping Max now as again she went to grab Liz who was slightly dazed. This was nothing to the pain she was about to endure.

"Please Max not like this."

"No this is how you like it isn't it? You like it rough. I've seen you in action, you whore, I've seen the film and slapped her you fucking lying bitch all these years you have been lying to me about you and Rose." Max was shouting now as finally her rage boiled over.

Liz didn't have time to understand what Max had said as she then started shouting obscenities at her, slapping her, punching her biting her. Again and again she hurt Liz appallingly as Liz begged her to stop once she hit her with the back of her hand with the diamond wedding ring catching Liz on the mouth; it bled immediately blood spilling onto the expensive sheets.

Liz didn't have the strength to control Max. Max had a new found strength which was frightening. She threw her around the bed harshly and she again hit her head hard on the wooden bedstead stunning her even more.

Max didn't stop as she ripped the vest Liz was wearing. This was now going further than it ever did things had never been as rough, hurtful as this.

"Please stop Max!" she cried frightened now for her life as again and again Max punched her in the stomach and face shouting at her all the time.

Meanwhile next door Mary seemed to have an intuition that something was not right.

"I need to go next door something awful is happening I know it."

She got up as Rose called her back. For once they had slept in the same bed.

"Mary leave it for goodness sake."

"No Rose, something is wrong I know it she seemed so sure of herself."

Her voice now troubled Rose as she too got up starting to worry she had never seen Mary like this. The fact that their relationship was in tatters did not prevent her from supporting Mary. Rose looked at her worried. She thought immediately about the CD and Max. She could tell by her tone she was very worried. As Mary went through the adjoining corridor she heard the screams and began to run upstairs shouting for Rose as she went.

Max's hands continued to brutalise Liz as she assaulted her all over her body. Once or twice Liz felt she had hallucinated seeing Sam and Rose in place of Max as again and again Max abused and violated her pushing her fingers deeper and deeper inside her as she finally raped her.

Liz begged her to stop, she was no match for Max's strength. Max was by blind drunk with drink and drugs as she was carried on hurting her again and again At the end of the assault as Max climaxed herself she bit a huge piece of flesh through her shoulder, the skin hanging off like a piece of dead meat. The blood poured from the wound as Liz shrieked in pain when almost immediately Max was pulled away by Mary.

She broke away horrified at what had happened, and backed herself into the corner of the room sitting on the floor pleading with Liz crying and screaming at how sorry she was begging forgiveness her hands bloodstained.

Rose arrived to the carnage.

"I'm so sorry, please Liz let me make it better let me help you," cried Max, shaking and terrified of what she had done crouching in the corner like a wild animal

Liz looked at her in horror unable to speak and then at the bed and her body covered in blood her particular nightmare had only just begun.

"Just clear this mess up you two!" shouted Mary as she gently and gingerly helped Liz to the bathroom. They burnt the sheets and blankets – the evidence.

"Not here," said Liz. Trembling her eyes wide with fright and the onset of shock

Somehow they got down to the gym and Mary helped her into the shower. Even now she was trying to protect her sister and she would ensure any DNA was washed away she could not have a crisis not at this time in her sister's career. She looked at Liz as she helped her remove what was left of any clothing and her heart at once went out to her – she knew how much she had loved Max and could see the devastation in her eyes. Mary helped her wash all the blood away all DNA being removed she thought of everything to protect her sister and helped soothe her cuts and bruises her shoulder still poured with blood and looked dreadful.

"Where's Rose?" she said quietly

"Listen Liz, I am the best friend you have at the moment I will look after you trust me," she said so gently and kindly.

Liz was in shock but not so much that she knew exactly where her mobile that Max had bought her was. She saw it on the pile of clothes in the shelving unit and somehow amidst all the mess began to make plans.

She then got into a hot bath that Mary had run. Mary helped her wash herself again and again and then gingerly held her as she got out of the bath. The only blood for now came for her shoulder wound.

"Will you be ok for a while? I need to check on the others and see what they are doing."

Liz shakily replied that she would be ok she needed a few minutes that was all to make arrangements.

Mary went to get the others and tell them they would have to talk to Liz that night. Max was not to be left on her own as she came down from her high. Rose was beside herself with a host of emotions about to erupt. The bubble had burst and it was all her fault.

It was then that Liz rang Peter and then Michael.

She spoke to Peter first. Her whole body pounding in pain He knew by her voice that something dreadful had happened.

"I need to get out of the country," was all she said, her head was excruciating.

He didn't ask any questions he knew by her voice something was very very wrong.

"Right," he replied, "get to Inverness Airport for eight am, Adam will be there and I will meet you at Newcastle. We will fly out to my villa."

"How many are going?" he asked gingerly

"Maybe three," she replied.

She then rang Michael.

"I am leaving the country something terrible has happened. Can you meet me at our spot at six am? I am not coming back I am going to Italy. Bring your passports I will look after you." That was all she said.

Michael turned to Sarah who by now was wide awake.

"Let's pack." As he explained the phone call and what he could make of it.

She was calling in a favour. They would tell no one their loyalty would always be to Liz they could trust her as she could them. It was two am.

Afterwards she began to try and get dressed as Mary came back. She prayed she had not heard her on the phone.

"Here let me help you."

Her face was enough to tell Liz she looked awful as the bruising was beginning to come out over her body. She helped to dress the wound with padding etc it was still bleeding badly and really needed medical attention by a professional.

Eventually they went back upstairs slowly and so painfully Liz could hardly walk and leant on Mary. Mary noticed how light she felt. It was by now about three in the morning and she had agreed to meet Michael and Sarah at six she had to stay awake.

The marks on Liz were appalling and Max was beside herself with embarrassment and grief at what she had done to her partner. She was no better than Sam she thought.

The bite on Liz's shoulder was still bleeding and beginning to look like it would go septic but Liz didn't care, her top half of her body was covered in bruises. Inside she hurt where Max had brutalised her. Mary continued to tend to the wound and tried to stem the bleeding.

Rose almost ghostly white began to explain what had happened all those years ago. Liz listened, she almost believed it was all a bad dream. She hurt all over but managed somehow to remain calm.

"Let me see the disc," she quietly said.

They put it on and after a few minutes Liz asked them to stop and give her a copy. She wanted to see it on her own.

For the next few hours all three of them apologised and explained why they had kept things from Liz all these weeks. Max did not speak at all. She just sat with her head in her hands crying trying to hold Liz's hands. Liz pulled away for her.

"I need to get my head round this on my own," she exclaimed, "and I need a drink." Mary poured her a brandy. She was going into shock.

Mary then told her the unfortunate thing was that Max in her drunken state had not seen the end of the CD when Sam actually explained that the CD was not her idea it had been engineered by two other people who had been supplying her drugs.

At the end of the day Liz had been the love of her life the most gentle and loving woman she had ever met and how sorry and appalled she was at her own actions and that she had been made to go along with it by two other evil people.

Liz didn't at that moment care if she lived or died yet again Sam had tried to ruin their lives. She felt betrayed and used as she had done once before. Although it was such a long time ago she couldn't understand why Rose had not told her. Rose explained that things just got out of hand and as time went on she just hoped it would blow over.

Liz was devastated that Sam had cheated on her and with her best friend it was almost too much to comprehend after what had just happened upstairs. It also did not make sense with the letter that had been sent it did not add up.

Instead when the letters came Rose had chosen to tell Mary and then Max. The three of them had known about this for about a month and had decided not to tell Liz. That explained why Max did not want to touch Liz let alone be with her and the longer this went on the angrier she got. They had wanted to ensure the book was finished so that they could all sit down together and discuss it rationally.

"But Rose you have lied. All these years and you never said anything. I trusted you with my life." Liz was heartbroken.

Rose just kept repeating that she was trying to shield her from any more hurt from Sam. Liz said nothing and just looked at Rose. Her deepest longest friendship was now on the verge of finishing. She looked at Max – her face said it all, she had made the worst choice she could. She looked at her in silence.

"All these years and I did not know. I didn't know Rose, you were my greatest friend, you have thrown it all away."

"Just imagine how Rose feels, it's just a shame she didn't tell you but then she was blackmailed not to!" cried Mary, supporting Rose to the end.

"That's how she was able to work for you."

Liz was devastated.

"But you chose to discuss it without me. I am your partner your wife. What about the drugs and the drink why did you take it?" she replied eventually quietly looking at Max.

"It's my entire fault," said Rose. She then explained what had been going on with the pills and the drink. It was all getting too much for Liz. All three of them had eventually betrayed her.

The night turned into day as Liz then calmly noticed the time. She quietly asked them all to leave.

"Please give me a few hours on my own; I will come to you later maybe we can talk it through rationally." Liz tried to sound as calm as she could.

The other three left Liz on her own. She now had thirty minutes left.

Liz was ready. She dressed in biker boots, commando trousers baggy t-shirt, dark glasses. She packed a small rucksack with her electronic notebook, some medication, passport and her personal bank cards. She left her ring on the table with her phone without the sim. No note. It was over.

She left the house by the side door and did not look back she would never live there again and tried to walk as best she could. She had often jogged this route and knew it would take exactly ten minutes to reach the road. She wore a baseball cap so that no one would recognise her at the airport.

It was light and the sun was up. Michael and Sarah were waiting in the car at the allotted time they had to be at Inverness by 8 and time was running out. It was getting close to six a.m. there was no sign of Liz.

They began to worry it was so silent and no sign of any movement. Sarah looked at Michael and was about to speak when they heard twigs crackle. Someone was coming. The noise startled them and they both looked up the small path. Ahead of them Liz was shuffling towards them swaying as she struggled to reach them. She held her hand out as they ran to her.

Michael stopped Sarah.

"Get back in the car and start it," he gently asked her.

He ran to her in a few strides and scooped her up like a small child carrying her back to the car.

"Help her!" as he put her in the back. He immediately got back into the driving seat and drove for all his might to Inverness.

Sarah immediately went into overdrive and began to tend to the hideous wounds as best she could.

No one spoke Liz just looked at her and quietly said, "Thank you."

Michael and Sarah were visibly distressed by what they saw.

"We are coming with you," said Sarah as Liz accepted some pain killers.

She was in agony. No one suspected next door she had gone. The least they could do was abide by Liz's wishes. They paced up and down Rose beside herself with worry. They made Max shower and cleaned her up.

Michael ensured they arrived safely at Inverness Airport where they were immediately ushered through. Sarah and Michael held onto Liz as she staggered once or twice. They were trying not to draw attention to the small party as they carried bags and got her onto the plane and met Adam. His face was immediately one of shock and horror as he looked at Liz.

"Help yourselves to anything," he said as he piloted the plane into the air.

They sat there in silence unable to comprehend the situation. When Liz had been so hurt by Sam he was not on the scene too much due to running the business for himself and Peter. It was only over the past few years her had grown to know and love Liz. He had a lump in his throat as he wondered what on earth had happened.

The plane landed at Newcastle and Peter joined them on the flight to his villa in Tuscany. Horrified at what he saw and the damage that had been done to Liz, he immediately get a bottle of brandy from the cabinet and poured them all a large glass. She did not drink on the plane however she just gently and unbelievably calmly told him what had happened.

He noticed bloodstains on the inside of her trousers and realised that this was something serious and not just a bit of horseplay. Her face was puffing up and bruising quickly. He still could not believe it. Sarah was concerned for her wounds and tried to soothe them and Michael just stared as the truth unfolded as his anger also grew.

He had begun to feel responsible for Liz and her welfare. He knew Max was wound up and tense but he hadn't realised how things were in the bedroom he felt almost responsible. The wounds were dressed as best as possible by Sarah and Liz at last began to settle more and as she started to cry, Peter saw the hurt and devastation in her eyes.

"I never want to see her again. Its finished I need to end it."

He knew by her tone she meant it. This was a huge mess and he needed to sort things out quickly before the press got hold of anything. He knew there would be calls from Scotland but his main concern was Liz he would do whatever she wanted. The rest of them watched her as they, one by one vowed to protect her for the rest of her life.

Peter knew her so well and he wondered if she would ever get over this. Thank goodness he had the forethought to call in a favour from his good friend Lucia. He always called her his number two girl. She would help.

They tried to relax for the rest of the journey. Liz slowly began to try to pull herself together. She was so hurt emotionally and physically but it was Sarah who noticed the steeliness in her beginning to from. The future was in doubt.

Chapter 20

Lucia

Lucia had known Peter since he moved to Italy almost ten years ago. She had in her younger days been a doctor of surgery and finally in the past five years she had studied Psychiatry. She was extremely striking and attractive with a very good figure. She was very intent on keeping her figure and worked out daily in order to keep it that way. She would be ideal to help Liz in another struggle in her life. In all the time he had known her she had never had a lasting relationship.

"I just analyse everything too much Peter," she replied, "it's better for me to be on my own and just have some close friends around me."

She had been in true unrequited love only once. The relationship had lasted about five years when her partner Bettina decided that enough was enough. Lucia was too much of a perfectionist and had begun to analyse everything about their relationship. The ending had been mutual and they had remained firm friends for years.

Eventually though Bettina moved to Rome and became involved with another man. That had hurt Lucia more than when their relationship finished but after much soul searching she realised unless she accepted the fact then they could not remain friends. It was tough for her and she took it quite badly as she said goodbye for ever. She vowed then that she would never fall in love again and risk the damage of that feeling of hurt once more.

Several women had turned her eye and she struck up strong friendships. These friendships would be for life. She adored women with a passion but would not allow herself to fall in love again.

She'd been involved with several women over the years but never wanted to take things further than just being physical. There was no way she was going to be involved in any more love affairs. Her heart belonged to her and no one else. She believed in friendships more than relationships. She often had close friends to stay and they always had fantastic times together but that was it. She had resigned herself to a solitary life and was more than happy with that. In fact she had not been with a woman for about four years and was quite content.

She was extremely wealthy, totally married to her job. She owned a villa high up in the mountains about an hour's drive from Peter's where she spent her spare time. These days she worked a couple of days in the week in a hospital in Florence. She was loyal and it was this loyalty that would be called into question when Peter brought Liz to Italy.

She was fun to be with, had a terrific sense of humour but above all she adored Peter and Adam and always said she should have had their babies if they had wanted any. She had no family to speak of and thoroughly enjoyed the peace and tranquillity of her home when she was there.

Like Peter she had a housekeeper and gardener who looked after her home when she was not there. Even though she was on her own she felt better when she had people around nearby. Maybe she was not that independent after all.

Chapter 21

Back in Scotland the other three women had kept their word and waited for Liz. At the allotted time she did not appear. Mary looked at Rose

"I'm going next door," there was no answer from the others.

Max had not moved from the corner of the room where she sat huddled up on the floor. Rose knew that everything was about to explode into a frenzy of hate.

Mary went next door and as soon as she saw the ring on the worktop knew Liz had gone. The house felt suddenly empty and lifeless. She had to remain calm.

She quickly went through the house and knew she had gone. She returned next door.

"She's gone," and handed her sister the wedding ring.

"We need to find her, she's hurt!" Max replied panicking.

Mary made some calls and realised that it must have been Michael and Sarah who had helped her. She rang Susan who was oblivious to everything. She knew Sarah liked her but she was not involved in this matter. She would have done anything for Liz but her loyalty had not been called into question not yet.

Max looked in shock still as they both looked at Rose.

"Tell me what happened Max? Tell me why you did this?" cried Mary. "This is such a bloody mess!"

The drugs and drink had begun to wear off for Max and she was now able to speak coherently now totally aware of what she had done.

"We need to find her Mary." she whispered desperately.

The anger in all of them was growing as they both turned on Rose.

"You have caused this you and your bloody pills!" cried Mary.

A huge vitriolic row then began between them, and then hatred reared its angry head as Rose bore the brunt of Mary and Max's rage.

"You may as well leave too," shouted Mary. "If all this stops Max I will come looking for you." She was so angry.

Rose looked at the woman who had shared her life with her for the past 7 years. Mary had come to forgive Rose for what had happened all those years ago but what she did not know was that she was dependent on these pills. This was the ultimate betrayal for Mary and was unforgivable. In her eyes Rose was responsible for what had happened.

"We can work this out Mary please, we need to find Liz. We need to stick together on this she's hurt goodness knows where she is." Rose was beside herself with worry.

Mary calmed slightly and realised Rose was right. Liz could now ruin everything. Even now Max was still her priority. They went round and round in circles until Rose eventually decided to leave. She packed her things then came downstairs as Mary looked at her her anger subsiding.

"No Rose, stay we need to work together on this. We need to protect Max from what could happen. We need to be united especially at this time in Max's career."

"I know Liz better than any of you," Rose replied. "She may well call the police. She may prosecute. God it's a mess!" and put her head in her hands.

Mary looked at Max and tried to decide what to do next. It had been the longest day and night of their lives and now she had to try to put the pieces together again. They had to remain as though everything was ok in the world.

In a few months' time the biggest exhibition of Max's life was about to open, her dream was about to come true. Nothing was going to stand in its way.

Max had ruined her marriage, been unfaithful to her partner, hurt her inconceivably. She hated herself even more than ever. She poured herself another drink although she didn't need any more.

She lit a cigarette she had not smoked back in Scotland but no one even commented. They were all in shock as they could not believe how much hurt Max had caused. Rose was beside herself with worry. Her first love had always been Liz and she too had hurt her beyond belief. It was all a terrible mess but they had to somehow hold things together.

Rose had an obligation to Mary she was still her partner but for how long she did not know. Her immediate thought was for Liz. She of all people had to repair the damage. Max had brutalised Liz and she knew deep down Liz would never forgive her. There was hope she thought that Liz would forgive her though. She looked at Mary so determined to protect her sister and she realised she did not belong there anymore. She still had feelings for Mary but she still adored even loved Liz. She was her priority.

Mary again took over.

"We need to stick together on this Rose. You must protect Max from anything that might be written about her. You need to contact Peter and speak to him, ensure that Liz will not call anyone about what has happened. I know Liz will not speak to either of us. I am relying on you," she sneered. "This is all your fault!" she spat.

Chapter 22

About six hours later the party from the plane arrived at the villa, Peter had rung ahead and his staff had got things ready. They were all exhausted; it had been a horrendous night and day. Sarah had found a pair of trousers for Liz the others were too bloodstained. Luckily the bleeding had stopped internally it was now the bite wound which was still oozing.

Lucia his very good friend had arrived and set to work on Liz carefully examining her. One look at Liz was enough to tell her she was in terrible pain physically and mentally. It was also a look to tell herself she was immediately attracted to Liz this was going to prove awkward. She was quiet and calm as she worked with Sarah to soothe her wounds. She had to examine her internally and was so gentle and reassuring that Liz hardly noticed what she was doing she was by now in shock.

"Whatever brute did this to you needs locking up," she said a lump beginning to well in her throat. She had heard all about Liz from Peter and felt she slightly knew her already. She had to keep it professional though it was so vital.

"It was my wife," she replied quietly as she started to cry silently.

Lucia suggested the hospital for the bite wound but Liz refused.

"Please can't you just stitch it up?"

"It will look terrible Liz, you need to see a plastic surgeon a huge piece of flesh needs to be cut away."

"No!" said Liz forcefully. "No more operations, no more. Please can you just deal with it?"

She sighed and eventually agreed to cut the flesh away and stitch it but the scar would be unsightly.

"Do what you need to do," Liz answered her it hurt so much but not as much as her heart which was broken beyond repair. "I don't care anymore."

Sarah knew she would sink into a depression now unless they all supported her. She knew Liz so well and this was by far the worst thing she had ever witnessed.

The four of them could not get their heads around the violence from Max. Broken – for the second time in her life. They sat up for hours discussing what was to be done.

Peter's phone rang again and again it was Rose pleading with him, begging him to tell her if he knew where Liz was. It went to voicemail she was beside herself with worry.

Eventually he went to another room and rang Rose out of earshot.

"I know what has happened Rose, but all I can tell you is she is safe. She doesn't want to speak or see any of you. Please don't try to find her." The exhibition was soon and the last thing Max needed was bad publicity. He had to try to protect everyone at this time in their lives.

Everyone was in a state of shock for several days. Liz's wound had turned septic and Peter saw to it that Lucia stayed at the villa so she got excellent medical attention with Sarah too. Not once did they go to the hospital Liz did not want that – another mistake.

Gradually Liz began to try to face up to what had happened. Michael and Sarah were already training again and she went over and sat with them. She knew she should begin to try to pull herself together her whole body hurt.

Peter looked at her as she walked gingerly to where the others were. He and Lucia talked amongst themselves and how they were going to try to help and support Liz through the next few weeks.

They were sure that slowly she would recover from yet another disastrous end to a relationship. As she sat she began to talk to them and told them she realised she had to pull herself together. Her speech was a bit slurred but they didn't seem unduly worried. They finished their workout and even suggested that she train tomorrow lightly. She agreed and then went to get up.

She felt dreadful and her head was splitting. As she stood a searing pain seemed to go through her head. She clasped it in both hands and screamed in agony as she fell to the ground. Michael and Sarah rushed to her with Lucia and Peter. Sarah and Lucia immediately checked her and called for Peter to get the car

She needs to go to hospital and now!" cried Lucia, now heavily concerned that they had not gone straight there on their arrival in the country.

Liz had suffered several blows to the head in Max's attack and this was now causing swelling in her brain. Things moved very quickly in the hospital and after several hours they were allowed to see her. The swelling had been attended to but she would need to stay in for several days. She was very ill.

Chapter 23

Max had of course had to be informed of this and had flown over she was the next of kin. They had finally got around to sorting that problem out after the attack from Sam. She was determined to win her back she knew she could if she really tried.

As she walked down the corridor Lucia knew immediately who she was. Again she had to remain professional but in no uncertain terms let Max know that she was lucky Liz was not going to prosecute. The others were with her as she went in. Michael and Sarah barely acknowledged her. Liz eventually awoke and looked directly at Lucia.

"Get her out of here please."

Lucia went to Max and ushered her out. As she did so she spoke to her. No one ever knew what she said but the look of horror on Max's face was enough to tell her she was in terrible trouble if she stayed.

Whilst Liz had been operated on the surgeons also took a look at her shoulder and tidied it up as best they could. She then left hospital after about a week this time well. She would heal psychically and vowed to train harder than ever. No one would ever hurt her again.

She would never fall in love again and allow herself to be hurt. She made this vow in front of the others and Sarah noticed the expression in her eyes was beginning to turn to steel.

Peter knew that Lucia would be needed to help Liz through this. He knew she would sink quickly into a form of depression she would need all the help she could get. If she carried on trying to act like a cool heartless woman it would hurt her too much. Lucia was the right person to help her mentally.

As her body repaired itself it was her mind that now needed help. Peter begged Lucia to help her and reluctantly she agreed. She was reluctant because deep down she knew this woman was going to play a huge part in her life. She knew that from the minute she saw her.

Eventually Lucia agreed she would help her to prevent any depression starting. She was slightly taller than Liz and very beautiful. For days on end they would talk about what had happened in Liz's life and she managed to draw on some memories Liz did not know she had thought her subconscious. The memories of Liz with Sam and Rose were brought to the surface at last, ironed out and left to dry.

She had never really understood the CD and what it represented she had never even remembered that evening until now and was sickened and appalled that the two most important people in her life had treated her like a piece of meat.

They had both betrayed her in different ways and she was devastated. When she had first watched the CD right through she was violently sick. How could someone who professed such undying love treat her like that?

Yet she had allowed Max to treat her so disrespectfully too. Maybe it was all her fault. It was strange to her that the two loves of her life had hurt her so much. Yes she decided it was her fault and she vowed to never fall for anyone ever again and ensured everyone around her knew how she felt.

They had all worked so hard on her mental state and slowly but surely the past began to feel distant. Liz at first was devastated and hurt. Now she was angry and feeling betrayed by everyone she had trusted. Lucia would spend a couple of hours a day with Liz unlocking memories and putting her mind at rest. Liz began to rely on her she began to get used to having her around. They were forming a friendship a bond that would never be broken.

As if that wasn't enough it was during this time that the first draft of the manuscript arrived. Lucia and Liz both worked together on it re-reading it. It proved to be something of closure for Liz. She was able to see just how much Max had controlled her with her sister and Rose. She was able to see just how much she had relied on them and how now she was going to live her life her way. Yes she had loved her with all her heart and Max had been a tower of strength for her when she was so ill, but she felt they never really appreciated the full extent of her recovery. She had never been allowed to be herself. She was now bitter and angry.

At last she was turning into the person she really was. She was training again with Michael and Sarah. She was finding herself and even slowly beginning to enjoy her independent life. She liked having Lucia around and was deflated whenever she was at the hospital. She had learnt how to live again how to enjoy life.

Peter and Adam were busy travelling all over and she was beginning to feel at home in Italy. She felt this was where she should be.

After about five months she was now clear of all memories. Her work done Lucia was more than happy to build on the friendship they had formed. For all this time it had only been Lucia who had been allowed to touch her.

Liz had been unable to let anyone touch her but now she was coming out of her darkest time and it was Lucia she was relying on more and more. She very rarely talked about Max, Rose and Mary now. In the six months since Max had hurt her so badly she did not think she would ever be able to forgive her.

She had instructed her lawyers to finally end the marriage. She didn't care if she never saw any of them again.

Lucia had to returned to Florence to the hospital but would call in on her way to her home in the mountain often suggesting Liz stayed with her for a few days but Liz wouldn't she felt safe at Peter's.

"Maybe one day I will," she used to reply there was always an excuse as to why she would not leave the confines of Peter's villa.

Michael and Sarah continued to stay with her and she now asked Michael to work out some routines for her. She trained daily in the hot baking sun. Peter had commitments which he could not cancel and was so worried about her. His work was overtaking his life and he was beginning to question just how busy he really needed to be. He needed to get off his own merry-go-round. He thought more and more about handing things over to someone else.

He really felt under the circumstances that someone else should be looking after Max. His loyalty was to Liz first and always would be and he did not like what he saw in Max anymore.

He saw to it that he left when she was in the right frame mind. She had all her hair cut short after her time in hospital and in the gruelling heat it had turned almost white. She worked out daily in the hot sun almost as if to punish and cleanse herself. She ate minimally and limited her drink even more.

She was working out for almost five hours a day it was too much he thought and yet the others were monitoring her closely. Lucia had begun to work out with them on more and more occasions herself a keen fitness fan.

They worked out together and slowly Liz began to learn to live again, Lucia was her mentor trying to bring her back to the life she once knew – they had formed a friendship and bond which would never be broken.

Chapter 24

Peter had a master plan for Liz's 40th birthday and now with all this tragedy at last becoming more distant in their memories it looked as though things might just work out.

Peter was looking after the refurbishment of the villa next door.

"I'm villa sitting," he remarked. "The owners have left me to look after things." But Liz made no remark. She was not interested in anything else other than her training. She was obsessed with her body now.

"It's all I have left Peter," she sobbed one day.

He now saw a side to her that he had never seen before and was worried. She seemed so far away from him.

"Liz is there really no chance with you and Max. She loves you beyond comprehension you must know that. After all you have been through don't throw it all away!" Peter remarked, he put the feelers out.

Her eyes flared. "I have nothing Peter, everyone has betrayed me. It's over!" Her comment stung like a barb.

He knew then that it was finished. Her eyes spoke of pure hatred towards Max it was then he knew he had to hand over Max to someone else. He was upset and felt a kind of responsibility as it was he who had introduced them to each other.

Peter, Adam, Sarah, Michael and Liz would have dinner most nights together when they were all there. They would talk into the early hours and often leave Liz and Peter talking until dawn as they unravelled more and more of Liz's fears and hurt. She was getting stronger by the day but she began to miss Lucia more than she realised but would not admit it to anyone.

One morning she looked very pensive. She had just done a gruelling run around the vineyard. She did this three times a week after training and she and Sarah would run together in the blistering heat.

"I need to speak to you Peter. I know you look after Max," it was the first time she had mentioned her name in a while. "Please do not stop working for her. This had nothing to do with your work. She and I are finished. I need to end the marriage I need to move on with my life. I am going to instruct my lawyers to hurry things along now. I need to start living again."

He looked at her and knew she meant it.

Not once had Liz asked him about Max. She had felt sorry for herself and only thought about herself and getting fit. She had become obsessed with fitness. He was so worried about how she was.

Although her body was looking good the best it had ever looked she was almost unrecognisable and her eyes had no expression in them. She had looked like that in hospital and he began to worry. She was punishing herself in the hot sun daily she would end up doing some damage to herself if she was not careful.

"Ok," he said quietly. "What are you going to do? Where will you go?"

He had noticed how she just seemed to fit in in Italy. She had not really left the villa much but she got on very well with the people who worked at the vineyard. It was co-owned by him and the owners of the other villa. He knew she had always loved Italy since before she went to London and met Sam.

"I have decided to make Italy my home I love it here. It is far away from Scotland and all that is there. I need to find somewhere for me this time."

He was relieved his plans could now come to fruition he thought.

"Well don't do anything until I get back, I will help you. I have something in mind," he breathed a sigh of relief maybe out of all the carnage his plan would be a success.

"Ok I will wait for you," and at last a smile formed on her face for the first time in all these months. Her face began to show less strain these days she was becoming content with her life and herself.

Chapter 25

As he disappeared she went to her room and switched on the computer. She had recently begun to email Scotland and then finally speak to Susan. As they spoke over the weeks Liz explained what had happened with Max.

Lucia had recommended she did not lose all ties. She knew they had slept together but was convinced that there was no threat from her. It was a purely platonic relationship and she noticed there was a pang of jealousy when Liz mentioned Susan's name. Susan had been there for her in more ways than one. And there were the horses her beloved horses to think about. Susan had taken care of everything at the stables.

She had been mortified as to what had happened but vowed not to tell a soul. She had supported Liz through thick and thin slept with her and fallen in love with her and would go to the ends of the earth for her, but knew deep down, Liz would never come back to Scotland.

"Whatever you want I will be there for you," she replied. Liz was already making plans to move the horses to Italy.

"I just need to find somewhere Susan, then we can move them over here and, of course if you would like to continue to work for me."

Naturally Susan agreed on the spot she did not have to think about it. She had not been involved in any way in the departure of Liz and that was one of the main reasons she had been allowed to stay in the business. Mary and Max had spoken to her and let her know her job was safe as long as she kept her mouth shut about any rumours that were beginning to spread. It was a tense time for everyone as the exhibition approached.

Peter arranged to meet Max in Scotland. He was dreading it in a way but he was their agent and business had to go on .The three of them looked awful but it was Mary who was looking after everything and everyone.

"We've got to keep up appearances Peter, Max needs to be in Paris in a few days this is her biggest exhibition since America. There's another exhibition in eight months. These meetings in Paris will be so important there are so many contracts that are up for grabs."

"What is more important, an exhibition or Liz?" he asked quietly.

Mary snarled. "Liz is the one who left us here not letting us know if she was alive or dead. I know what my sister did was unspeakable, but we have to carry on. This is our dream about to come true, she should have made more time made more allowances for Max."

He sensed then that Liz was right it was over.

"I need to talk to Max," he replied.

"Max I need to speak to you about Liz, she has told me it's over and is determined to finalise the end of the marriage."

Max looked at him through bloodshot eyes and he noticed the scotch and pill bottle next to her.

"What are these?" he asked.

"They are mine," she snarled. "Mine Peter. No one else's. I know what I did was terrible, but I know I can win her back, I always have done."

He looked at her his anger beginning to boil he was appalled. He was so cross and upset all at the same time this was not the Max he knew and he didn't like what he saw one bit, but he continued to try for his own benefit to prove to himself it was over.

"Then you'll have to quit the drugs. I know what you have been doing, don't think I don't know," he replied. He was calling her bluff and it worked.

She looked surprised she thought no one knew she was addicted to these prescription drugs the ones that had caused all the problems.

"Don't take me for a fool, isn't that what got you into all this mess? You haven't learnt a thing, you have just thrown everything away. Liz adored you, gave you everything and yet now you throw it back in her face. You are worse than Sam."

His anger now got the better of him as he defended his greatest friend. Tears welled in his eyes as he carried on telling her of all the hurt she had caused. He knew then it was really over.

"Yet again I have had to watch her putting her life back together again after someone she loved so much with all her heart has hurt her. Do you know what I think? I think you hurt her even more than Sam did. When Sam hurt her she was under sedation for months so that she never felt the raw pain that she caused. With you it was so real. I saw the pain in her eyes, I felt the pain in her heart. We all put her back together again, all of us, and you will never get close to her while we are around her. We are her safety net."

He carried on with his tirade. "You have your art the thing you wanted most in your life, you have what you and your sister have always wanted. You will soon have the fame and the money it's what Mary wanted for you. You have everything.

"You even pushed her into marrying you, do you really think that is what she wanted? Even now you still keep Marianne dangling. Whilst you declared undying love for Liz, you betrayed her so many times in Paris. Liz hadn't even thought about betraying you and yet here you are kidding yourself that there is a chance for you two.

"Well, let me tell you now Max, leave her alone don't hurt her anymore." There he had said things he wished he'd said a long time ago.

She looked on as he carried on telling her life story. She had to agree with him. Her own jealousy had in fact ruined their relationship. She had smothered Liz with love and caring after Sam had hurt her so much. She had been there for her throughout the whole time of her recovery and yet not allowed Liz to be her own person.

The problem was that as her fame progressed she got more commissions. This is what caused the tension and pressure between the two of them. She had been selfish in their relationship eventually.

It was very one sided her taking advantage of Liz. At first she was so gentle with her but eventually it was too one sided. She wondered if she had pushed Liz too far. Had she really wanted to marry her? She knew with her drinking too much she had taken advantage of the situation many times pushing Liz into making hard, fast almost violent love so many times. In fact she realised how like Sam she had become and she now at last hated herself for it.

He was beginning to calm down now as he saw how upset Max was becoming. Quietly he carried on.

"Get some help, do something to bring the old Max back, the Max we had all loved."

He looked at Max. She looked awful, bags and dark rings under her eyes, scotch next to her. He knew her so well though and knew that her painting would be brilliant but that her mental state was probably in a terrible condition.

"She doesn't need help; she has me and Rose to protect her for the outside world. We need to get through this to put her where she belongs at the top." Mary had walked through and yet again interrupted her sister.

Peter realised there were a lot of issues here that would take a very long time to iron out.

"Well, try to clean yourself up, you will be in demand for interviews and you need to give the appearance that all is well."

He was dreading the next few weeks. They all needed to be sure that she didn't say or do anything else to provoke more news headlines about her relationship and addiction.

Peter and the three women were travelling to Paris the following day, Peter had sorted out the travel arrangements and they met Adam at the airport as they prepared to fly out there. The mood was sombre in the plane and he was relieved when they got to the hotel.

He would look after Max as best he could, but knew deep down that he could never forgive her for what she had done.

The three of them all attended meetings and interviews and spoke to reporters all of them carefully avoiding the question of where Liz was. Marianne had been contacted by Max immediately they arrived and ensured she was in the background so as not to attract any further publicity they were a polished act and no one would have guessed the truth behind the facade they were putting up.

Dinner was a quiet affair with Mary, Rose, Max and Marianne. Peter was busy with organisers and ensuring everything was perfect for the next day. Mary did not approve of Max and Marianne being open about their relationship but dare not put up any fight – Max could be on the verge of exploding with the tension that was building. Rose and Mary left the pair of them realising they also had to try to work on their own relationship whatever that was nowadays.

They talked for another hour or so until they began to reminisce about the past. They both knew they were on dangerous territory and were as bad as each other. What had happened in the months before the wedding they agreed had been a mistake but Max kept repeating to Marianne she was a free agent now she was getting a divorce.

"Nightcap?" said Marianne. She knew that Mary and Rose would not be back at the hotel for hours.

They left the hotel and walked the 30 mins it took to get to Marianne's vast house. She lived on her own now. Max marvelled at the paintings in her house and noticed some of her own work that she had kept. Her house was just superb perfectly emulating Marianne's style – bohemian like Max. As they continued to talk the subject changed from other things to Liz.

"Do you want Liz back?" Max looked at Marianne with a puzzled stare.

"What I did was despicable. I would not blame her if she did not want me." She looked so forlorn.

"Do you love her?" she asked quietly. "Do you love her Max?" she repeated the question.

"Yes of course I do, I always will but…" She paused. "But I will always love you Marianne."

They looked at each other in the eyes and then Max made her move. They had had a lot to drink and for both of them all cares were thrown out.

Marianne responded not once refusing Max as she continued to kiss her, hold her caress her more stronger and harsher than ever before her

"Slow down Max not so fast we have plenty of time," whispered Marianne.

They moved to the bedroom and for the next few hours took each other back in time to how things used to be. Max had not been with anyone since that dreadful night and was at first scared of what was happening but it was Marianne who put her at ease and together they explored each other after all these years taking each other to incredible heights of ecstasy again and again.

As they lay there together afterwards they did not speak both unsure of what the future held for them. All Max knew was that she had also betrayed her soon to be ex-wife yet again. She wondered what would happen now. Deep down she knew it was probably over between her and Liz and for the first time since that night she cried as she held onto Marianne.

Chapter 26

The long awaited exhibition had opened to huge marvellous reviews for Max. Their dream had come true.

The success they had all dreamed of for Max came immediately as soon as the exhibition opened. She was a star. Mary was in her element as Rose watched from the sidelines realising their biggest dream had come true. Max was paraded round like a prized animal in a ring and loved the attention. Over the next few days she attended interview press releases and TV shows. Mary and Rose looked on protecting her from anything that could get in her way.

All the years of hard work that Mary had put into this moment had now paid off. She watched in admiration as Max somehow managed to fool everyone into thinking she was well, healthy and did not have any problems. Rose looked on and realised it was time for her to now finally leave the twins and her partner. She and Mary had carried on living under the same roof working hard for Max. Now her work was done.

As they celebrated her success she looked at Mary the woman she had loved so deeply and knew it was time to go. They had agreed to keep up the appearances of a happy couple until the exhibition and Rose knew it was now time to go and to try to make amends to her dearest friend somehow get her forgiveness.

As she walked away she breathed a sense of relief the pressure had been immense these past few months and she was so tired of

Scotland and the twins. She did know where to start but her thoughts were to also find Sam.

The ending was an amicable relief for the pair of them. Almost relieved Rose walked away not once regretting the split.

Chapter 27

Peter had flown back home for a few days before he was due back to Paris for another round of interviews for Max. Rose had left them and he needed to ensure that no harm came to Max. He also wanted to ensure that Liz was fine and asked Lucia a favour.

He spoke to Lucia quietly away from Liz.

"You know she has her yearly check-up don't you? I was wondering if you could look after things I need to get back to Paris," he questioned her.

They agreed that Peter and Adam would take Liz to the hospital and after all of the tests Lucia would drive her home. Lucia then began to make some plans.

"Of course I will I would do anything to help her you know that," Lucia replied.

Don't hurt her Lucia I can see you are very fond of her.

"I would never hurt a hair on her head. We are just friends Peter." She was slightly annoyed at him.

It was the only way Peter could think of them getting her to the hospital as she did not drive and Michael and Sarah had returned to Scotland to pack up their home. They had decided to move to Italy– they would follow Liz anywhere in the world wherever she decided to settle.

"Have you remembered Liz's birthday is next week? It's her 40th you will be here won't you?" she asked him.

"Of course I have remembered but I cannot get out of this. I really need to hand over the ropes I want to spend more time with Adam and now I have to miss her birthday. You'll look after her won't you? Will you do something special?" His eyes pleaded with her, she saw how sad he was.

"We'll just get away and enjoy the time together Peter. Do you have any plans for her?"

He then began to tell of his big plan and she looked at him.

"Don't tell me anything else Peter, I don't want to keep secrets from Liz she has had enough of that."

"You're right," he replied, "but it will be the best present she has ever had," and winked.

"To be honest I don't think she has remembered it's her birthday anyway. I'm not going to make a big thing about it as she will miss you two so much if I do."

"Just don't let her fall in love with you just yet."

She seemed stunned at his remark.

"I don't know what you mean," and dismissed the comment, "but I do wonder if in fact her heart belongs with Max, Peter, I think it belongs elsewhere that much I can tell you."

He looked puzzled and then decided not to ask any more questions. He was frightened in a way he had never felt before. Maybe all this soul searching was too much for everyone who knew where it would end up.

"We'll go up to my place and we can do some walking and riding all the things she enjoys. Just take it easy, after all she has not really left your home in all these months."

Peter was immediately worried as he could see Lucia was falling for Liz. Liz was particularly vulnerable but he trusted Lucia even so as he left he just said to Liz quietly, "Be careful don't let your heart get broken again."

Liz was puzzled Lucia was a friend and nothing else. Peter went to the hospital with Liz where they met Lucia. They said their goodbyes and Lucia took over.

This was the first time that Liz had not been in Scotland for her check so everything was new to her. New specialists and doctors were now looking after her. The morning was gruelling with a lot of tests and questions. She felt good after the tests and then finally had a meeting with an analyst who delved into her private life and thoughts. She was used to this after all her time with Lucia and was happy to chat away. Her Italian lessons had proved to be useful as some of the talking was done in Italian.

At the end of the morning one question remained in her mind and would do for several days.

"How long have you been in love with my friend Lucia?" the analyst asked.

She was taken aback by the questions and finally had to admit to herself that against all odds maybe she had fallen in love again. She was also surprised at some of the other things that had been said. She would talk to Lucia later as she was trying to get her head around some of the statements that had been made.

Lucia also was talking to the specialists about Liz. One of them she knew very well and she too was slightly dumbfounded as they said goodbyes.

"Does she know you are in love with her?" he questioned her.

She looked shocked at her friend. "You're in love with her right? After all these years Lu I have never seen you like this."

Lucia had thought she had been able to keep her feelings hidden but it seemed there were only two people in the world who did not know what was going on and that was Liz and Lucia.

They drove back to Lucia's villa. Liz was very quiet and thoughtful after the long morning. Lucia put the top down of the car so they could feel the hot sun on them. She looked at Liz several times as she looked so pensive.

"Your results were fine so why the thoughtful face?"

They told me some things I didn't know. I suppose I didn't realise how controlling the others had become. It's as if they took my identity away."

"Maybe they just didn't want you to hurt yourself again they were thinking of you," she replied gently. "That time has gone now you need to look to the future."

"There was something else they said," as Liz looked deeply into her eyes.

Lucia was frightened of what Liz was going to say and changed the subject. She had to get her own head around things too.

She pulled the car up and they looked at the wonderful view as they had climbed further up the mountain.

She reached over Liz slightly, "Look," she said, "you can see Peter's house from here." Their faces were so close that if Liz had turned they would have kissed.

Instead they just looked at the view both wanting each other. Liz did not know what was happening to her but certainly something was stirring side her.

They arrived at Lucia's villa and once there Lucia made herself busy with her housekeeper.

"Just make yourself at home," she said quietly. "I won't be long I just need to sort out a few things."

Liz walked out onto the terrace looking around the wonderful views. She began to relax and think about what had been said to her today. She was very fond of Lucia and couldn't imagine life without her playing some part in it. She began to realise that the hospital was right she had allowed herself to fall in love with her but was terrified of rejection. Liz began to relax and think about what else had been said.

She began to look at Lucia in a different way and realised that the hospital was right. She daren't say anything to Lucia as she had always made it quite plain she did not want to fall in love again. She was terrified of being rejected. They both were. They had both told each other they would never fall in love again

That evening they sat and chatted and began to relax with each other. They both realised they were looking at each other longer than normally but did not dare say anything. Lucia showed her to her room it was large and airy with a view looking down onto Florence itself. She was tired and welcomed the thought of a good night's sleep.

"We can do whatever you want tomorrow just get a good night's sleep," and with that she was gone.

Liz slept heavily and did not stir all night. The next morning Lucia knocked gently on the door

"Hi, how are you today, how are you feeling?"

"Hello," replied Liz. "I'm good thanks."

"Great how about a workout, swimming and some horse riding then?"

Liz jumped at the idea and within half an hour they were both working out on the terrace. They finished with a swim and then both of them changed. Lucia leant Liz some clothes and they set off to the nearby stable.

Lucia noticed how sexy she looked in her riding gear. Liz felt as if she had been released from a dark place as for the next few hours they rode, laughed, chatted and thoroughly enjoyed themselves. Everything was relaxed between the two of them but deep down the tension was building from both of them.

Lucia too had things to think about after the hospital. She flatly refused to fall in love and yet here she had to admit at last that she needed to tell Liz what she was feeling. She too was terrified of rejection as in the past months in their conversations they both admitted to each other that they did not have any intentions of ever falling in love or indeed trusting any one ever again.

That evening over dinner they again chatted about mundane things and laughed Liz hadn't laughed in a long time and she was thoroughly enjoying herself at last.

In two days' time it was Liz's birthday although she seemed totally oblivious to it. Lucia decided that they would go out for a nice meal in the nearby village higher up in the mountains the evening before.

It was about half an hour's drive and much higher up. Very exclusive and very expensive.

You may need to borrow some of my clothes," she remarked as she explained that she had booked a table. She had plenty of clothes and Liz could have a look to see which she wanted. Liz wasn't sure if she really wanted to go she was more than happy at Lucia's but after some gentle persuasion she realised Lucia was right she needed to start living her life again. She was after all used to the finer things in life.

They had spent the following day similar to the previous one. Liz was used to a routine and if broken she could become slightly panic struck. She still had some way to go before she was properly well but the improvement over the past weeks had been marvellous.

On the day of the meal they spent the afternoon riding again and afterwards there was a need for a long shower before they left for the restaurant. Lucia lent Liz some of her very expensive shower gel as they both went to their rooms to get ready.

Liz was thinking long and hard in the shower about Lucia and once out put on a robe and went across to her room. Lucia was at her wardrobe thumbing through clothes, herself fresh out of the shower – the room smelt of the delicious scent of it. She tapped on the door and went in.

"Hi, here's your gel back... wow!" she explained and headed straight for the balcony. "This view is amazing. It's totally different from the one in my room," she enthused.

She stood looking out as Lucia came to her

"Yes you see how different it is it overlooks Peter's villa? This room is the other side of the house look there's Peter's villa. You can run to it from here see the path," and she pointed to the path.

The drive took about an hour from Peter's along the winding roads but you could run from villa to villa in about fifty minutes at a pace.

She looked at Liz as she pointed their faces very close this time. She took in the fresh scent of the shower still on her skin. She could smell the freshness of the shower on her and moved closer towards her.

Liz looked round at her to see Lucia's eyes almost boring a hole in her. She had an ache in the pit of her stomach as she looked into her eyes.

Lucia moved towards her and kissed her gently on the mouth.

"I'm sorry," she whispered. "I shouldn't have done that I…"

Liz stopped her in mid-sentence by responding to her kiss equally as gently.

They then looked at each other with a knowing look and kissed each other passionately as their emotions began to kick in. Liz's body felt as though it was waking up, but this time waking up to the touch and feel of Lucia.

Lucia broke away. "Are you sure? Are you really sure?"

Liz just looked at her, her reply was another kiss. They began to kiss again their bodies at last touching passionately. All these months of passion had now come to an end as the two women held each other.

"Don't be scared my darling, I will never hurt you."

Tenderly and gently Lucia caressed her and whispered to her ensuring her making sure that that this is what Liz wanted.

"Are you sure?" she whispered reassuring her again and again.

She was frightened herself of overstepping the mark. She helped Liz take her robe off as she took her own off expertly as she led her to her bed.

Their bodies were at last naked together as Lucia gently stroked and kissed her in a way Liz had never been kissed before – never before. She gradually and slowly rediscovered Liz's beautiful body telling her how much she loved her.

The two women were expert and experienced lovers and now at last they were together.

Lucia gradually began to reawaken Liz's body gently and carefully not rushing. Liz began to relax more and more as Lucia showered her with gentle kisses. She explored her body with her hand and tongue as Liz began to respond.

"I will never hurt you my love, as long as I have breath in my body," whispered Lucia. "Let me love you, I have wanted this moment for so long."

She began to kiss her as Liz relaxed more and more to her touch and kisses. Gently and slowly Lucia began to kiss her all over her top half of the body. This time the hands that touched her were gentle and loving. This time the kisses were meaningful. As her hands touched her breasts they were gentle and teasing. Her mouth began to travel all over her. Liz stiffened up once or twice but Lucia constantly reassured her and she began to relax again.

Her hand then began to travel towards her thighs they were both already near the point of no return but again Lucia tantalised her.

For a very long time they explored each other's bodies and then eventually Lucia's hand again began to travel towards her thighs.

She stiffened again but Lucia relaxed her with such sweet words. Eventually her hand met its target where she began so expertly to tease and tantalise her almost to the point of ecstasy and then she would stop. She had awakened Liz's body and now she knew the time was right to totally fulfil her.

Liz cried as she climaxed again and again. She had never known such passion and was taken to a point never experienced before. She gasped and cried out again and again until she could take no more.

Her whole body shuddered and she held onto Lucia as if she would never let her go smothering her in kisses again and again and then for the first time began to respond to her lover in a way never before.

It was now Liz who treated Lucia to unbridled passion expertly ensuring she was fulfilled in the same way. For hours and hours they experienced ecstasy at its highest level finally exhausting each other into the early hours of the morning as again and again they cried out as they fulfilled each other telling each other how much they loved one another. There was no rejection they both felt the same.

They finally slept heavily entwined with each other and hardly moved. Eventually a few hours later it was Lucia who woke first slowly. She looked immediately at Liz as she slept and for the first time realised how beautiful she was.

She knew how Max had often woken up Liz and took her immediately and the last thing she wanted was for Liz to be reminded of that. Her whole being excited her and she kissed her shoulder. She stirred inside and looked straight at Liz who now awake responded to her kisses. Liz began to kiss her everywhere and so gently and as her tongue moved lower down her body Lucia began to arch her back for her.

Her tongue licked a trail up her inner thigh until it reached the point where Lucia cried out as again and again she fulfilled her with her tongue. Eventually she moved to return the compliment to Liz as she in turn cried out again and again. Finally totally spent out they fell into a deeper sleep as the dawn began to break.

Around mid-morning as they lay there Liz spoke first.

"Well I guess they cancelled the table automatically," and laughed.

They were so relaxed with each other and their eyes were so full of love for each other a love neither of them had experienced for many years. They lay in each other's arms quietly and relaxed. Lucia eventually looked at Liz and kissed her holding her closely.

"I love you Liz," and kissed her.

Liz looked at her. "I love you too Lu, I really do…" and they held each other.

There had been several missed calls on Lucia's phone from the restaurant and they decided they ought to ring and apologise. It was no problem and they rebooked for another night.

Lucia looked at Liz and realised she still had no idea of the day.

They were totally at one with each other and it was Lucia who spoke first.

"I'm sorry but I have to say something Liz."

Liz immediately looked worried there was no stopping Lucia.

"I realise now I have been in love with you for some time and I cannot imagine you not in my life. I know we both said we didn't want a relationship, but I do love you Liz and want to spend the rest of my life with you."

There she had said it. Liz looked at her tears welling in her eyes.

"Lu I love you so much, I feel exactly the same I never want to lose you ever," and held her tightly.

They laughed and held each other close. For the moment they felt like the only two people in the world and they did not want to lose that feeling.

They kissed each other again and again and indulged each other in passion insurmountable. Once again they exhausted each other and afterwards Lucia spoke softly to Liz

"Oh there's one more thing," she looked at Liz.

"Happy birthday, my darling."

Liz looked at her and then worked it out

"I hadn't even thought about it."

"I know that's why I booked the restaurant. I wanted you to enjoy your last night in your thirties," and smiled.

"I will never forget it," she replied and smiled as she kissed her again longingly and deeply.

They were gentle and passionate with each other and knew instinctively how to treat each other. It was the sort of lovemaking that Liz had been craving for a long time and she was not going to let it go. Lucia had awoken her body let her trust again let her enjoy another woman's body again she adored her.

"Come on," said Lucia, "let's go the terrace and have some champagne."

They eventually got up and went for a swim first. On getting out they sat on the double lounger as they dried themselves and then took each other again. They both felt a huge release after the past few months as their feelings for each other had begun to change. Sooner or later they would have to attend to other more pressing matters like Max and the divorce but for now the remaining days of their holiday they were going to thoroughly enjoy themselves and each other.

They had a fun 10 days in the mountains and Liz felt so alive at last. They both worked out and swam. Lucia was very keen to stay in shape. She was three years older than Liz but she was perfectly toned.

Lucia's villa was smaller than Peter's but in a way far cosier. It had a small gym area outside and a fairly large pool more than enough for what they needed. The evening sun shone brightly each night on the terrace where they would sit and watch the sun go down,

They drank and ate frugally as was Liz's want. They began to laugh as well and Lucia looked at how much progress was being made with Liz.

They didn't do anything different just enjoyed each other's company. They went horse riding and Liz enjoyed it so much. They went walking. Liz had made such a leap forward and had finally managed to shake off the depression that had been hounding her.

Not once did they take each other for granted they just respected what they had between them. A bond had formed which would never be severed. This bond was something Liz had never experienced before and she loved it and not once did she consider that she had been unfaithful to Max her marriage was over.

They returned to Peter's villa feeling alive and so much in love. This was different for Liz, she had never experienced this sort of feeling before.

This was a different love stronger than ever before. There were all sorts of arrangements to be made she needed to find somewhere to live.

Lucia knew Liz needed her own home whether they would live together they did not discuss at the moment they just wanted to spend as much time as possible with each other.

On their return they did not profess or admit anything to anyone. They didn't have to Peter knew immediately they had at last realised they were in love with each other but did not make a big thing about it. He carried on as normal totally accepting the situation. He was so happy for them both his special ladies.

Chapter 28

Peter had to break the news that Rose had arrived to try to patch things up with Liz. He thought she would be annoyed but she announced she would listen to Rose and what she had to say yes she was healed.

He spoke to Lucia who proudly looked at Liz and casually remarked that the annex was to be used by Rose and that he presumed she would move into Liz's bedroom. They laughed as they all realised this was a new beginning for the two of them.

Rose had flown out with Peter to see if she could retrieve her friendship with Liz. She would be staying in the annex away from the villa. There was no way he would have them all under the same roof. Rose and Peter watched Liz for over an hour in the searing heat as she pushed herself to exhaustion again and again with weights and press-ups. She knew her so well and yet she did not know how to begin to talk to her. Peter would take over the situation. She looked on totally mesmerised by the sight of Liz. He knew then she was still in love with Liz. He watched her as she drank heavily from a bottle of wine. She told him it was to steady her nerves.

Eventually Liz and Lucia arrived back on the terrace having showered. Liz wanted Lucia with her at her side. They began with small talk and immediately Liz could see Rose was not at all herself.

"I only did it so as not to upset you I knew how much you loved Sam it would have broken her heart if you had known about the other women and the drugs." It was a pathetic start from Rose after all that had happened.

"If you had told me then we could have dealt with things. You chose not to Rose and I find that so hard to understand – maybe just maybe Sam wouldn't have driven to Scotland and half killed me." These were the most profound words she had ever spoken.

Lucia in her brilliance had drawn memories and feelings out of Liz that she did not even know she had. Michael, Sarah and Lucia stared in amazement. Suddenly the weight lifted from Liz's shoulders she would no longer blame herself for what the two people she had given her heart to had done. For all the shame she felt she realised it was not her fault. Her confidence was now second to none.

"But Liz, I wanted to shield you from Sam. Please Liz."

Liz's eyes told her she would not back down.

"At the end of the day Liz I was looking out for you, you have to forgive me at least I didn't rape you." The others gasped.

"But you did Rose, in your own way you did." She looked at Peter.

Rose then began to shout at Liz, realising she had ruined the situation that could have been repaired. By now the drink had kicked in, too much again Peter thought as she had polished off nearly a whole bottle of wine within the past hour. The brutal vocal attack continued upsetting everyone in earshot.

"You're nothing, you're spoilt all these years we have had to pussy foot around you. I have hated Sam all these years because of all the terrible things she has done to you. You and Max together were a bomb waiting to explode can't you see that? I worked so hard to keep everything afloat, ticking over I worried daily about you especially towards the end I know how much she hurt you. Don't think I don't know what went on in the bedroom Mary told me. I have always loved you Liz always, I did all this for you and yet you still love Sam I can see it in your eyes."

Calmly and quietly although terribly hurt Liz replied, "No Rose you are so wrong, I did love Sam and I did love Max." She automatically held Lucia's hand without even looking at her. "But now I have found my true love and no one will ever come between us. Remember Rose, there is a very thin line between love and hate. We're done here," she turned and walked away from them.

Peter called Liz to stop and started to follow her. Lucia held his arm gently.

"As Liz said we are done here," and caught her up as she reached the end of the pool.

She put her arm round her and the two of them walked through the gate to the vineyard to be alone. She was so proud of Liz she had been so brave and she knew she must be upset.

Liz's anger slowly began to subside as she realised where her destiny lay. She adored Lucia and wanted her by her side for the rest of her life.

Rose and Peter talked for a long time about what had just happened before she left for England bereft. She had so wanted to make things right with Liz instead she had made them worse. She vowed to Peter she would stop drinking and would track Sam down to sort out that particular problem with the cd. She was determined to put everything right between her and Liz and get her forgiveness.

Eventually the two women returned and Peter spoke to them both. He apologised profusely about the situation with Rose. He knew the two women's friendship had been so deep at one time. He also knew Liz had been very fond of Rose depending on her with her life at times.

He hoped for their sake they could eventually find a way to repair what had broken. He just wanted Liz to be happy and content. His big plan for her belated birthday present was about to come into fruition nothing was going to spoil that. For the next few weeks the atmosphere went back to how it had been before Rose's arrival and he realised he had never seen Liz so happy with her life.

Chapter 29

As if to add insult to injury, Max arrived in Italy for one final showdown a month after the exhibition had finished. Rose had contacted the twins; they were still on speaking terms and had explained what had happened on the terrace. Max was staying in Florence with her sister and Marianne. She had the fame and fortune and a new confidence about her. Whatever she wanted she had.

She had rung Peter and explained she needed to see Liz one last time to see if could salvage their marriage. She had heard from the lawyers and was determined to win her back. He was furious as she arrived unannounced. Adam was beside himself as they had only just seen the back of Rose and all was returning to normal.

She marched through the villa onto the terrace where everyone was exercising. They had almost finished their training for the day. Immediately she noticed how at home Lucia was with Liz and realised that the two of them were intimate with each other.

"Who is that other woman Peter? Is she the doctor who was with Liz? She looks familiar," her voice was calm and gentle.

"That other woman is Lucia, she has helped Liz get to where she is now," he replied softly.

Peter did not lie. "Max leave it, she's happy with her life don't spoil it for her, if you really love her let her go," he was panicking now this could turn into a brawl.

The wheels were set in motion to end the marriage, Liz was happier than ever and now here was Max larger than life.

"Hey Liz I'm back!" he called to her.

She was soaking wet with sweat, and so lithe it scared Max. She looked powerful in her tiny frame. No one would ever overpower her again this was not the Liz she had married. She watched as Liz undressed and dived into the pool in a bikini she powered her way up and down the lengths for almost 20 minutes. If she was doing this sort of workout each day then she was mad.

Michael and Sarah worked out with her and she noticed how at home they all were together. She felt an outsider as she looked on realising that the love of her life had begun to rebuild hers, and she was not part of it.

The heat was well into the forties and there was no shade other than the veranda. As she came to the end of her swim Peter picked up a towel and held it out for Liz.

"Hi you," thrilled to see him but then looked further on and saw Max.

Her eyes then went cold and dead. The scar on her shoulder was a reminder of her violence towards Liz. As she gasped in horror, Max knew then that their relationship was in tatters. Liz had a new found strength.

"Can we talk Liz please?" she asked quietly almost frightened of the answer.

Liz looked at her with an expression no one had ever seen before, it was one of pure hate.

"What about Max? What about? How you have betrayed me? How Rose has betrayed me how you abused me? Hurt me? Violated me? How you raped me? Where do you want to start?" she almost hissed.

Lucia and the others looked on not saying a word, this was Liz's fight. She had a new found power which frightened Max. Deep down Max hurt so much. All too often in the past if things were getting difficult they forgot about it all by going to bed this time it was so different.

"There's nothing to talk about its finished," she replied calmer.

"We have so much history Liz, don't throw it all away I know what I did was unspeakable," she was begging now. "Please Liz please!" she cried.

Liz looked at her and for a split second Lucia thought Liz would waiver.

"No Max, for months I went along with whatever you wanted. I supported you in whatever you did, but then you repaid me with this," and she pointed at the scar. "You will never touch me again."

She looked further to Peter and said quietly, "I said it was over Peter."

Max went to towards her to hold her; the others made to move towards her which frightened her.

"No it's fine I will go," realising that it was over.

There would be no more conversation it was finished she knew that now. For a moment she had thought she would be able to make things right again. She had cleaned herself up stopped drinking and had stopped taking pills she was clean. She had mistakenly thought there was a future for her and Liz how wrong she was. She walked away from Liz as Adam appeared.

"I've called a taxi it will take you back to Florence." As he passed her he said quietly, "Don't ever darken these doors again, be thankful she never prosecuted, you still have you fame and fortune."

Max was astounded and shocked as well as upset. This time she was gone. The meeting had taken less than thirty minutes. In that time Max realised at long last it was over.

She had everything she wanted but in the end she had nothing. Yes she was in a sort of relationship with Marianne but deep down it was Liz she wanted more than anyone else in the world and she realised that if she did want Liz back she would have to try a different way. She did not care how long it took she was determined to be in her arms again.

Chapter 30

After the upset of the situations with Rose and then Max, Peter decided it was time to give Liz his belated birthday present. The timing was right now. Everything was complete and Liz had seemed to have made huge steps since the situations. He was amazed at her and realised how much work she and Lucia had put in. She was stronger than ever mentally perhaps she now had closure and could get on with her life.

"Let's go the villa and looked at what's been done there," he excitedly asked the pair. Lucia and Liz had no idea what was to happen.

"Come over tonight and have a change of scenery," he continued.

Later that evening the four of them walked to the villa next door which took about 10 minutes through the vineyard. It was a slightly smaller villa than his.

"Wow!" exclaimed Liz as soon as they entered.

She felt strangely at home apparently 'the couple' who owned it had spent a fortune refurbishing it and now Peter had overseen the completion. The truth was that Peter had purchased the villa almost three years ago and had spent this time refurbishing it to a certain style and taste – the style and taste of Liz.

This was to be his project for the next few years which would culminate in Liz's 40th birthday it was not on the market but at the moment Peter was not giving out that information. He had to be sure.

"Well what do you think?"

He showed them over all of it and watched for Liz's reactions. By now Lucia realised what was about to happen and ensured she kept a back seat. This was Liz's moment and she looked on realising how much she loved her.

Liz adored it and he knew she was thinking seriously about moving to the area. It was all so perfect. He showed them the bedroom the huge bed still in its wrapping it must have been seven foot square. He had thought of everything he knew Liz so well.

"Well what do you think?" he casually asked.

"It's beautiful," she said replied. "Just beautiful!"

"Could you live here in a place like this?" he carried on.

Lucia stood back as Liz accepted the most wonderful birthday present from Peter.

He then went on to explain.

"Sit down Liz, I have something to tell you. You remember the money you lent me all those years ago while you were with Sam?"

Lucia and Adam looked on bemused. They knew Liz had amassed a fortune of her own but never knew how much, they just knew she was a millionaire.

"Well, with interest, this is what my accountants have worked out how much I owe you. I always said I would pay you back. This here is a breakdown of how much I have spent on this villa to refurbish it and furnish it.

"It is my birthday present to you. The amounts I owe you and what I have spent are about the same. If you really like this villa here are the key and the deeds. I just don't want them signed to you until your divorce is through so Max cannot have it. If not I will just write a cheque with interest for what I owe you." By now everyone waited as they watched Liz take in what had just been said to her.

Liz was dumbfounded. She could not speak as the enormity of what Peter had just said began to hit her. She was almost hyperventilating as Lucia held her and calmly told her to breathe.

Now Liz knew why he and Alan had looked so smart the previous couple days ago they were at the lawyers. Liz couldn't believe it and of course said yes. She loved the place. The timing was right. Liz was ready to live her life again she was healed. She called Michael and Sarah and they came over as quickly as they could.

"Plus as I know you get bored and you have to have something to do, there is a small matter of the vineyard to run, no one has looked after it properly for a few years. I know you love it as you use it as a track every day to run round!"

There was a smaller house in the grounds which she would give to Michael and Sarah who had been so faithful to her. She looked at them and immediately offered them the property.

Sarah and Michael for once were speechless. The evening was emotional for everyone.

Eventually Peter beckoned them. "Come in here," as they all went to the kitchen, "I was banking on you saying yes," as he opened the fridge. All that was inside now was champagne. Adam had taken care of some food.

They moved from one room to another taking everything in again. Then they went to the house that she had given to Michael and Sarah and marvelled at what he had completed in there. Not once did Liz feel everything had been done for her behind her back. She had trusted Peter for as long as she could remember and she marvelled at the magnificent gesture and time he had spent. She held on to Lucia's hand as she tried to comprehend the enormity of what had happened over the past hour.

Later that evening they began to tidy up.

"When are you moving in then?" Peter laughed.

Liz's eyes were wide with excitement and happiness.

"Tomorrow if possible."

They decided to share Peter's housekeeper and gardener it made so much sense.

Finally the happy group went back to Peter's knowing that the house would be spotless again tomorrow not that they had left any real mess. Liz was fanatical about tidiness now having been apart from Max.

As they walked back Liz as always automatically held Lucia's hand. Everyone was buzzing about the new life that was now laid out in front of them. Lucia knew Liz would not be able to sleep with excitement her head would be busy with plans she just knew it.

They all settled on the terrace with a nightcap and gradually went to bed. It was two in the morning. Liz and Lucia sat next to the pool and looked at each other.

"Looks like I have found my home," said Liz and kissed Lucia softly on the mouth.

Lucia took her hand and they walked to Liz's bedroom silently. There was no need for words.

Once inside they held each other tightly as they began to kiss each other hungrily. Again and again they took each other to paradise when eventually they fell into a deep settled sleep.

The next morning they woke together and smiled at each other. They kissed each other it was Lucia who spoke first.

"Hello my darling," as she held her gently.

"Hi," replied Liz a bit sleepily, she had drunk far more than she should last night.

"Are you ok nothing is wrong is it?" Lucia seemed to worry immediately.

"Just a bit sleepy," she replied as she responded beginning to caress her.

"You've got to get yourself moved today, we have to get you awake," smiled Lucia.

"I know what I'd rather do," she replied huskily and again she took Lucia to ecstasy. They professed undying love for each other surprised at how easy it was for them to talk about their feelings. Nowadays Lucia marvelled at Liz's body as her lover rather than her doctor. Hours later they showered as training was cancelled everything was so relaxed.

There were too many loose ends that Liz had to tie up before they could contemplate a future living together although they knew that was their destiny. They did not have to mention it they were meant to be together and were so thankful they had taken their deep friendship to a higher level. Lucia's villa in the mountains would be a welcome retreat for them eventually where they could take themselves off for a few days at a time to be totally alone. There was so much planning to do for them both. Lucia held onto Liz and together they realised they were entering into another phase of their lives.

Peter could see they had such strong feelings for each other and he hoped with what was to come these feelings would conquer all. It seemed Liz and Lucia were the only two people who had not realised they were falling in love with each other and he smiled to himself. His wonderful ladies were now settled. Later that day everyone helped Liz move in.

"It's not like I have a lot of stuff," she laughed. It all fitted in a few boxes.

"We need to get some clothes for you, you'll be doing interviews and photo shoots soon once the book is published." Lucia would ensure they would purchase some in the near future.

As the day turned into evening they all excitedly prepared a meal in Liz's kitchen. The atmosphere in the house was happy and full of laughter just how Liz liked everything to be. Michael and Sarah had also begun to move into their house and after dinner spending some time on the terrace everyone began to leave leaving Lucia and Liz alone at last.

Liz looked at Lucia she stood up and took her hand.

"Come," she said quietly taking her hand. "Let's go to bed."

Her first night in her new home would be spent with her new love Lucia. Lucia stood up and kissed her longingly as they made their way to the bedroom. Liz felt at home for probably the first time in her life. The pair of them had never known a passion such as theirs and continually marvelled at the way they made each other feel. Throughout the night until the early hours of dawn they made passionate love not once doubting the love they had for one another. The last piece of their jigsaw in life had been placed it was perfect.

Chapter 31

Rose had flown back to the UK after the disaster in Italy with Liz. She booked into a hotel in London and began to think about Emma and Sam. She made various calls and planned the next day. She knew she had to sort her life out and sort out everything with Liz. She could not forgive herself for what had happened and vowed to make amends.

She easily tracked Sam down she was living in the grounds of her parent's estate. The next day she travelled down to the countryside and a few hours later arrived at the large home of Sam's parents. She had rung ahead to see how the land was lying speaking to Sam's mother who seemed almost thrilled she had contacted her.

Sam was born into money. Her parents were a lord and lady and lived in a lavish house and grounds in the heart of Sussex. She had two elder sisters who she aspired to. Throughout her life she had been spoilt always getting what she wanted. She was volatile and temperamental and would go through a majority of her life at full speed. How alike she and Max were.

She knew she preferred women from an early age and had several relationships whilst at boarding school. She didn't know at that stage in her life what she wanted to do. She could have worked on the family estate if she wanted but her elder sisters were involved in that.

She wanted to make a name for herself in her own way and took a shine to cookery and organising parties. Her parents decided that she would go to the best hotel school in London and soon set about organising her flat where she could live throughout the term.

They would fund her throughout college determined that she would succeed but very conscious that she should make a success on her own and without their influence. They adored their youngest daughter and yet worried about her temper. She would work hard on that in her later years but well after she had made a huge mistake in her life.

"Sam will be thrilled to see you she has not had any visitors since she came home," her mother remarked.

She got in her 4 wheel drive and asked Rose to follow her. They drove for a mile or so in the grounds and then arrived at a wooden lodge. Liz would have loved this thought Rose. After all these years her first thought were always Liz. They walked to the lodge and Sam's mother called out to her as they went in.

"Sam there's someone to see you," she called as they went through to the back of the lodge.

Sam looked up from the garden where she was digging and started to walk toward the lodge. Rose gasped silently when she saw her. She looked so like Liz her hair was cut short she was wearing a vest and shorts. She looked frail and pale. Her eyes were sad but they brightened up almost nervously when she saw Rose.

"How wonderful to see you!" She seemed genuinely pleased to see her as her mother left them.

"I'm sure after all this time you have plenty to talk about, call me if you need anything darling." Sam's mother gave her a knowing look – she was looking after her daughter.

"Welcome to my home," she said in almost a whisper and ushered her back in.

"Forgive me Rose, I am a terrible host. Have a drink, what will it be?"

"Whisky will be fine," replied Rose as she remembered the last occasion Sam poured her a drink what had happened.

"It's ok it is just whisky," said Sam almost sensing what Rose was thinking.

They talked for hours about this and that and what Sam had been doing. She had been released from the hospital after four years the last two spent as a day patient. She had then spent the next two years living, working and studying in a nunnery. This was not the Sam that Rose knew.

"It was part of my treatment to try to put something back into society it was my rehabilitation," Sam explained.

She had been living here in the lodge for about three months, back home under very close scrutiny from her parents. They had ensured that her finances were looked after. In fact Sam was quite wealthy in her own right.

"I have learnt such a lot about myself and just wish I could turn back the time," she said so quietly.

Rose looked on as her pent up anger was slowly beginning to subside. She got up and offered Rose another drink.

"What time is Emma back?" asked Rose matter of factly.

"Emma?" she asked. "Emma? Oh you mean that Emma."

"You know," hissed Rose. "Don't play games with me Sam." Her own anger getting the better of her. She breathed heavily and deeply she had to control herself.

"I haven't seen Emma since that day in Scotland, she was pure evil Rose. She got me to do some terrible things," she replied quietly and calmly but truthfully.

Suddenly things became so much clearer to Rose. Emma was behind the disc and probably much more. They carried on talking for hours and eventually Sam suggested something to eat. She carried on talking as she prepared a meal for them both.

She was visibly upset about what had happened between Liz and Max.

"My God! I would never wish any more hurt on her. Emma was a huge mistake but I was just so stupid and got myself into so much trouble. I allowed myself to become involved in a very dark period of my life which, in turn, ruined everything and the woman I really loved."

"Tell me about Emma," replied Rose her voice much calmer as she could see how upset Sam was becoming.

Sam began to explain how she got involved with Emma and another woman called Chris. They provided her with drugs to just give her a lift art first but it was done for a reason to get back at Liz.

As time went on Rose realised the words Liz had spoken about love and hate were true. The woman she had hated all these years she now was beginning to see in a very different light.

It was now dark and getting late and they had talked long into the early hours of the morning.

"Please feel free to stay the night I have plenty of room," it was a suggestion from Sam.

Rose stayed the night in the guest room and after about an hour she heard crying and gasps. She didn't know what to think was going on and turned over and went to sleep. She remembered vividly how Sam and Liz's lovemaking was often very vocal.

The next day they carried on talking it was as if it was a therapy for Sam. Rose had already decided to track Emma down and explained to Sam of her intention. Sam was at first nervous and then thought it would be a good closure for everyone concerned.

Things needed to be sorted out and a legal step taken if necessary as it was blackmail in a way. If the press got hold of it there would be an outcry. What had up to now been kept behind closed doors could engulf all of them. Rose continued to make plans and calls from Sam's home.

Rose had noticed how she limped sometimes and asked what the problem was

"Oh just an old war wound," she said not looking at her.

Rose let the reply pass, it was not her business.

She had been staying there for a couple of days as they made their plans when she decided that maybe Sam would like a run out in the car. She began to see the softer side to Sam the side that Liz said she never saw. The kind gentle side drink and drugs free and she realised liked what she saw.

"It will do you good to get out and have a change of scenery," remarked Rose.

"I don't know Rose, I haven't left this place since I got back. This is all I know."

How like Liz she was now. Liz had not left the house in Scotland very often preferring to stay at home working out or writing that was her life. They drove out for a couple of hours and Sam realised how wonderful it was to be alive again. She never thought she would see Rose or Liz again this was a fresh start. She looked at Rose and she liked what she saw.

"Do you realise this is the most time we have spent together and been civil in all these years. It has been wonderful."

"Yes," replied Rose. "What a lot of time we have wasted hating each other."

They drove to the coast and walked for hours talking laughing and both beginning to wipe away their dreadful memories of each other. This was a new start they could begin again and become friends.

It's what Liz would have loved to have happened all those years ago thought Rose regretting so many things.

They spent the next few days together again talking and growing fond of each other. It was a closure for both of them and they realised the one thing they had in common was Liz. She was the most important person in this trio and matters had to put right. She had to know the truth and why things had happened the way they did.

The next morning Sam had an even worse limp and looked awful. She struggled in the kitchen and Rose was immediately worried.

"What is it Sam what is wrong?" she cried.

"You'll have to help me," she gasped. She lifted her shorts to show a steel garter pulled tightly round her leg. She had learnt of self flagellating in the nunnery.

Rose looked in horror as she helped her to sit down.

"It is there to remind me of the evil pain I have caused."

Rose now realised how troubled Sam was over how much hurt she had caused Liz. This was the noise every night and not what she had thought at all as she tightened the garter more and more except this time she could not undo it.

"My God Sam, what have you done to yourself?"

She struggled at first but eventually helped to get the garter off to reveal terrible cuts in her thigh. She gently bathed and cleaned Sam up and made her vow not to ever use it ever again.

"I will get rid of this monstrosity." She had put some gel on the wound and the healing began again for Sam.

They sat together afterwards with Sam still in a lot of pain but eventually it began to subside.

"Sam listen to me," begged Rose. "Liz has forgiven you I am sure. Her hate and anger has subsided over the past years. She often talked to me about you and how things went wrong."

Sam looked at her with such sad eyes. "Do you think if I wrote to her and explained?"

"No, one thing a time, Sam. I have had a dreadful argument with her, I have to put matters right between us and then explain about all of what you have told me – trust me I think I can fix it."

"I can't imagine you and Liz every rowing Rose," Sam replied knowing that she would write to Liz and explain everything.

This time it was Rose's turn to talk and she told Sam everything that had been said on the terrace back in Tuscany.

"So you see I have lost Liz too, but I am sure we can put it right one day. I regret so much the things I said to her and I miss her so much."

"Are you still in love with her Rose?"

"I realised a long time ago she will never love me like I love her. I loved our friendship but ruined that in the end. Not a day goes by without me regretting what we did Sam." They were both upset.

"Then let's put it right once and for all I will work with you – we can get this fixed I'm sure, let's work together Rose, we both still love her in our own way."

"Now to business. I need to go to London and track Emma down. Will you come with me?" Sam winced as she started to get up.

No, I need to get this leg sorted and just take stock of things. I would rather be in the background of things Rose, but I will help however I can. Besides I can't leave the garden it is my work but I will be waiting for you to come back. Hey listen to me putting gardening before business." They laughed gently both still unsure of each other.

All these years of hating each other had taken their toll and now they needed to work on building a few bridges and become friends again.

Chapter 32

Rose went back to London the following day to find Emma. It wasn't hard as she had good connections still through their businesses. She needed to see Emma for herself to make her see what she had done what damage she had caused.

Max's work was being written about photos were taken but there was none of Liz in any of them. Time was running out for them to keep putting up the excuses and the papers got the inside story the divorce was written about. The paparazzi were beginning to put two and two together about Max and her temper and the complete disappearance of Liz. The word was out.

A few phone calls were made to her contacts. Eventually after a large amount of investigating over the next few weeks Emma was charged with blackmail. The story had to be kept from the press even now Rose was trying to protect Max. She realised her loyalty to Max was still there and she need her forgiveness too. The fraud squad were brought in and Emma was ruined. She had been squandering huge amounts of money to satisfy her drugs habit. She had a partner called Chris who had been involved with her for years.

It was these two women who had been in bed with Sam when Liz walked in on them all those years ago. That was the one thing that Liz had never remembered fully. She knew when Emma worked for her she seemed familiar but just could not put her finger on where she knew her from. She had successfully put that memory away never to be relived again.

Rose bought out the company quickly and quietly. She had the financial means and she had a fantastic business brain. The PR Company that Emma was running could be turned into a very lucrative company and in turn would prove to be very successful. She knew working alongside Peter she had the means to turn everything around and reunite her with Liz. She knew Liz would never take Max back but at least it could be a start with her and Liz.

She was away longer than she thought but rang Sam almost every day giving her updates and letting her feel part of the process. Chris the other woman in involved with Sam had engineered the whole thing. Before Sam and Liz got together she had a date planned with Sam before they both started at college.

Chris had seen her around the complex when they were having their interviews. She introduced herself to Sam and was immediately bowled over by her. Everything was arranged for her to go out with Sam and the evening was a something of a success but Sam wasn't really interested in her.

She became dangerously infatuated with her. She had built up in her mind a relationship that did not exist. She was mad and very dangerous a first class meddling bitch who would stop at nothing to get what she wanted. She would trample over people and their feelings to get her ultimate goal.

She had followed Sam for the next few weeks and was desolate when Sam went abroad for a holiday before she started college. She became besotted with her. She despised Liz as it was obvious to everyone that once Sam saw Liz she wanted her and wanted to be with her. Liz was in the way and as the years followed she plotted her revenge.

She recruited Emma on the act and between them they planned to bring down Liz. She had taken her Sam away from her. She hated her. How long the revenge took only resulted in how much damage she was able to do to Liz – damage that would affect her for the rest of her life.

Rose relayed all this back to Sam over the phone. Sam could not even remember her before college she just remembered that terrible morning when Liz walked in on them she had never forgotten that.

Eventually Rose wrote to Liz. It was a letter full of apologies for what had happened. It was pages long as she begged her to let her explain the reasons behind why she did what she did. She begged for them to meet up and explain everything. Liz read the letter several times. She had read a great deal lately as she was ploughing her way through the completed manuscript. Lucia and the others had all read it and were amazed at her writing. It was perfect and the book would be published and on the shelves very soon. Liz spoke to Peter and Lucia about Rose.

Rose called Peter and this time he listened. She explained what had happened and he gradually relented as his brain went into overdrive. If Liz would accept Rose's apology then Rose could be the perfect person to run things again. They met and discussed the matter in London. They spent hours discussing what had happened, Peter gradually realising that things could be retrieved if handled carefully.

He rang Liz and explained what had been discussed and was pleased to hear that she would see Rose. Liz was so happy in Italy with her life and he had never in all the years he had known her seen her so relaxed with everything.

It was perfect and this time she agreed to see Rose with Peter. They waited for Liz and Lucia as they walked through the vineyard together. They looked so relaxed and carefree and Rose could tell that Liz was finally at peace with her life. She watched them as they climbed the steps to the terrace. Liz looked so well now. Her eyes had sparkle in them. She was a woman in love a true meaningful love.

She listened as Rose explained everything to her and took it on board and began to realise the sorts of pressures that Rose had been under as she worked so hard to help Mary in her quest for dominance in the art world for Max. Yes it was a terrible shame that she had found the drugs but in the end it was not Rose who had raped her.

Yes she should have told her all those years ago but somehow she was able to accept Rose's explanations as to why she did not. What had happened between Sam, Rose and Liz was many years ago and unless Liz could forgive her there would never be a friendship again. They agreed to meet again the next day at Peter's and Rose watched them as they walked back to Liz's home arm in arm.

Lucia was with her and Rose could see how in love they were. She had never seen Liz like this before relaxed and totally at peace with herself. Rose warmed quickly to Lucia and eventually Liz began to forgive her for everything.

Lucia knew she would and was happy that Liz and Rose seemed to have closure. She asked about Sam and how she was quite matter of factly and any doubts Lucia had were soon overcome as Liz continued to profess her love for Lucia. She felt no pangs of worry or concern as she knew Liz was honest and truthful with her. They agreed to try to put things behind them and Rose was thrilled that her beloved Liz was beginning to forgive her. In fact Liz had missed Rose very much but they needed this time apart to work out their friendship.

Chapter 33

Rose had been away from Sam for about five weeks. They had been in contact most days just talking about the day and Sam was thrilled for Rose that she and Liz had begun to retrieve their friendship. She knew Liz was such a forgiving person.

Sam welcomed her back with a tight hug and they looked at each other intently as Rose kissed her on the cheek.

"I've missed you," she said as Sam responded,

"I've missed you too," replied Sam looking into her eyes. Eyes that were soft and full of gentleness and love a love that Rose craved. Eyes that were drink and drug free.

They held each other tightly not letting go and then their emotions gave way as they kissed each other again. This time on the mouth gently and passionately they gave way to their emotions and all the years of hatred. Their hands and mouths explored each other carefully and gently releasing a host of emotions.

Sam had always been an expert in the bedroom and knew instinctively what Rose wanted as she kissed her more and more passionately.

Rose was excited beyond belief and responded as Sam took her hand as they made their way to the bedroom. Neither of them had been in this situation for a long time especially Sam and yet she knew exactly what to do. Sam was an expert lover.

Rose remembered much later that Liz had said only a few months ago before the brutal attack from Max that no one could love her the way Sam had. She would never forget those words. Rose allowed herself to be kissed and touched passionately and gently by Sam.

She responded to her every move and their bodies were perfectly in tune with each other. Sam kissed her longingly as her hand moved over her body exciting her beyond her wildest dreams. They were perfectly relaxed with each other and took each other to the limit in passion as they both climaxed almost together. Exhausted hours later they lay together contemplating what had happened between them. They were quiet and held each other closely. It was Rose who spoke first – even now Liz was in both their thoughts

"Liz was right you know there is a very thin line between love and hate."

Sam looked at her and kissed her. "This is the right time for us, maybe we have had to go through the other stuff to bring us to here to this point in our lives."

She had fallen for Rose. Not in the same way she had loved Liz that could never be repeated. Liz had always been the love of her life and every day she regretted what had happened between them. She realised she had to get her forgiveness too.

Rose knew that after all these years that Sam was the one for her she couldn't believe it as Sam told her how much she had fallen in love with her. They talked and talked how their feelings for each other had been re-awoken after all these years. Although Liz had forgiven Rose they now needed to tell her about what was happening between them and soon.

"We will tell her but in our own time, let's not run before we can walk," said Rose

Sam knew she was right and agreed they needed to work on what was growing between them before they had any more confessions from the heart. They needed to be sure of each other as they began to enter into a relationship neither of them thought was ever possible.

The next few weeks were busy with Rose setting up the business and Peter helped. He liked the way she worked and was beginning to think about Max. If things could work out then perhaps Rose could act for her.

Rose was particularly happy. Her split from Mary had been sad and sorrowful both of them realising it was the end of the line. However Rose had agreed to help in any way she could for the sake of Max and somehow in between all the mess of the break up they managed to salvage a friendship of sorts. Mary could not handle Max on her own and Rose still had a loyalty to them both. She had loved Mary truly but as the years had gone on they had drifted apart. Their relationship towards to the end was one of friendship.

The night of Max's attack had changed everything and she had stayed on long enough to ensure that the attack was kept out of the press. They had between them protected Max's reputation ruthlessly and this was where she had been able to show her true strength in the world of PR...

The divorce had been mentioned as quietly as possible in the press and no one had been hurt by anything.

Mary had continued to have her base at the house with Max living next door as she had done. Max was a handful still and eventually she had contacted Marianne who had flown over and stayed with Max. She knew their relationship was reignited and just was thankful that there was someone else to shoulder the burden of her. She often thought about Liz and what a terrible time Max must have given her. She now realised how much Liz had suffered as she would often talk to Marianne about her temper.

The longer time went on the more she thought about Liz and vowed to one day try to repair the friendship between them. She too needed closure with Liz and set about trying to come up with a plan that would make this happen. She knew there was a chance of seeing Liz again as Peter had told them of his plan to hand the reins over to Rose. She was now running a very successful PR company and if they agreed to it she would handle Max. They trusted Peter and realised he needed his own space and agreed that if Rose would represent Max then they would be happy with matters. Everything was working out for the better at long last.

Chapter 34

Peter decided he was going to offload some of his work – it was if he was retiring. He wanted to spend more time with Adam. He spoke to Liz and Lucia and explained his decision and they thoroughly understood.

He already had in mind a PR company that would handle their work. It would be Rose. He had always kept in touch with Rose and having made arrangements the next thing was to let Liz know. It was only right that they were honest with each other and that Max would be looked after by Rose. He would ensure he still looked after Liz but Rose would be handling most of the work and promotions.

He explained to Liz what his plans were and as they had put things right between them she agreed it was probably for the best. It also meant Rose would be looking after Liz when the book was promoted. Liz trusted Rose and knew she would be perfect for the PR work. It was what Rose did best.

It also gave them an insight into the way Liz thought and they all agreed that Liz was a woman who could forgive the worst possible thing. They all sensed she had feelings still for Sam. It was going to be a merry go round once the book was published.

They knew there would be interviews wanted and wondered if Liz would be able to handle the pressure. He would always be there for Liz and would never ever let her come into any danger again. He would see to that. He and Rose just needed to ensure they worked together for Liz. There was also danger that she and Max may meet again.

Rose and Sam were now heavily involved in their relationship and Rose felt it only right to let Liz and Peter know. She was dreading telling them but they both knew that sooner or later the word would be out. Rose flew to Italy and spoke first to Peter.

He was quite surprised at the turn of events and quickly agreed that Liz needed to be told. If she did not want to be managed by Rose he would take those reins back. It was down to Liz. There was a photo shoot involving Rose for the publicity shots for the company and time was running out she so wanted to tell Liz herself.

By now Lucia and Liz were more or less living together. Lucia was working so many days in Florence which gave them their space and when they were together it was magical. The relationship suited them both.

Rose rang Liz from Peter's and they agreed to meet at his villa for a meal that evening. Lucia and Liz were puzzled as to why there seemed to be a need to speak to them and could not imagine what on earth it was about.

Rose had brought some copies of the magazine with her and over dinner began to explain how she had met up with Sam again and how they had become very fond of each other. She then tentatively announced that they were an item and waited for the response.

Lucia watched her partner take a breath and then quite calmly announced that she was happy for her dearest friend and wished her all the luck in the world with the relationship. She was so proud of her as she continued to chat to Rose quite matter of factly. Rose showed them the magazines photos.

At first Liz was stunned then after lot of thought realised that perhaps at last Rose had found what she as looking for. She thought she had no feelings either way until she saw the pictures. She looked at Sam how she had changed her appearance and realised she had very similar looks to herself. She looked at the woman she had loved with all her heart and was amazed at the feelings she still had.

She held Lucia's hand as she spoke as usual.

"I have found my soul mate Rose, perhaps you have found yours I truly hope you have." The rest of the evening passed pleasantly as they all seemed to sense a relief now that everything was out in the open.

Lucia began to relax as she really believed in Liz what she had said to Rose. As they walked back to Liz's home they talked a little about Sam, things needed to be said and put to rest once and for all. Peter and Rose watched them as they walked back together. Peter noticed the body language was not quite right between them.

There was a possibility that Sam, Max and Liz they would meet up at some stage in the future with Rose managing them all and Lucia had a nagging doubt in the back of her mind.

"You're quiet Lu what is it?" asked Liz concerned.

"I just wonder if you really still are in love with Sam that's all." There she'd said it her eyes full of worry.

Liz looked horrified and was desperately upset at what Lucia had said.

She held Lucia tightly. "Please Lu, don't think like that. I love you I have never felt like this about anyone else it's you I love please don't speak like this."

There was a chink in the armour a doubt in Lucia's mind and Liz was mortified. She was upset and now Lucia realised she had overstepped the mark. She hated herself and wished she could have turned back the time. She just had misgivings about Sam and what the future held for them.

She held Liz as she explained in more depth. Lucia explained that she worried that Liz would forgive and fall back in love with Sam. She knew Liz better than she knew herself and she knew that Sam really was the love of her life or had been. Liz looked at her through her tears and saw the worry in Lucia's face.

"Then Rose will not manage me it's as simple as that. Peter will remain my manager it's not a problem my darling. She will never come between us I promise you." She rang Peter from the vineyard he had watched them and knew she would call. He guessed what the problem was and he and Rose were more than happy to let Peter continue to look after Liz. There was also a kind of relief from Rose.

Lucia had let her guard down and upset Liz she hated herself. Liz was still upset when they returned home and they spent some time talking about Sam before Lucia took her to bed to ensure Liz that everything would be alright. For Liz the seed of doubt had been sown. She loved Lucia with so much passion and she cried with her for ages as Lucia herself assured her it was a one off moment of doubt and would never happen again. She kissed her and Liz responded they loved each other so much and it looked as though Liz had forgiven her for that one remark.

Liz was surprised at Lucia's lack of confidence and began to understand how she might feel scared at the thought of Sam entering their lives again. Lucia had seen the look on Liz's face when she saw the photos and it had bothered her. The tenderness in the eyes frightened her.

They adored each other without doubt but Liz was concerned at how fragile Lucia could be. She held her closely as she slowly began to kiss her all over her body telling her how much she loved her. Not once did she think about anyone else Lucia was her world. They spent hours making love and reassuring each other that they had nothing to worry about. At last in the early hours of the morning Lucia realised that Liz meant every word she said and she hated herself for having mentioned Sam. They lay there together and she was so upset she had hurt Liz she would not mention it again she had to learn to trust Liz and believe her. She wished she had not made the remark about Sam.

Lucia had a course at the hospital and would be away. Liz wondered if perhaps that was why she felt vulnerable. They would be apart for two weeks. It would prove to be a very long time for the pair of them to be apart.

Chapter 35

The couple spoke regularly over the phone. They missed each other so badly and Lucia especially was desperate to see Liz again. She wished she had not said what she had and worried herself about it. She wasn't sure if having this time apart would make Liz re-evaluate their relationship. This was the sort of doubt she had had in her other relationships and she hated herself for it.

On the final day she drove home to her own villa. She needed that time on her own. She was a mess mentally and did not want Liz to see her like this.

Liz had been busy that day at the vineyard and although very disappointed agreed they would see each other the next evening. It had been a horrible time for them both. Sarah and Michael knew she was upset and tried their best to encourage her to be bright and hopeful about the situation.

The next day she finished her training then spoke quietly to Michael and Sarah and explained she was going to run to her villa. She couldn't wait until the evening. At first they decided to go with her but it was Sarah who said she needed to go on her on. They knew she would be safe and would wait for her call when she got there. They could see she just wanted to be with Lucia. They ran some of the way with her then after about 40 mins turned round and came back home.

She arrived at Lucia's villa. She was sitting on the terrace with some books and a bottle of wine had been opened. She took in the scene as she stood still out of breath slightly hot dusty, and a small cut on her leg where some brambles had caught her. She didn't feel it at all, all she wanted was Lucia and her love. She had missed her so much.

Lucia had been looking over the terrace and saw in the distance someone running up the path which led up the mountain. She fetched some binoculars and saw it was three people. On closer scrutiny she realised it was Michael Sarah and Liz. She was so excited and immediately went to the kitchen and found some more wine which she put in an ice cooler.

She sat and watched and then realised that the other two had turned and returned which left Liz running up on her own. Michael had rung Lucia and got her to watch out for her. Liz was safe.

"I'm sorry Lucia, but I can't do this anymore. I can't live like this. I love you and no one else you have to believe me," as the tears ran down her dusty face.

Lucia looked at her and held her realising she had jeopardised their relationship with her own inadequacies

"I thought I'd lost you. I love you so much too. I am so sorry for saying those things for doubting everything please forgive me." She kissed her passionately as they held each other as if they would never let each other go.

They tried to speak to each other amongst the kissing but it was no good. They made it as far as the double sun lounger where there and then they took each other to a place of no return. There was no one else near the property and they were totally alone. They laughed they cried they spoke to each other as equals as they both realised that they could not live without each other. Whatever life threw at them they were a couple.

They jumped into the pool and laughed as they kissed each other again and again realising how frightened they had both been about their relationship and Sam. Eventually as the sun began to go down they settled down to an evening together to talk about the future and what it might hold.

Now her divorce was through her villa would be transferred into her name with Lucia. This surely would prove to Lucia that Liz was totally committed.

"Is it too soon to ask you to marry me?" whispered Lucia. "I mean I know you are just divorced, but do you think you could consider about it?"

"I don't need to," she replied. "You know my answer is yes." And she kissed her again longingly. They were back together where they belonged and any doubt had been removed. They could not live without each other.

With Lucia away Liz had thought long and hard about her home and the spare land at the end of the vineyard. She made a decision to have stables built and then spoke to Susan in Scotland offering her a job. She made enquiries about her beloved horses then left Susan to make arrangements to have them transported out to Italy in the near future.

All ties with Scotland were being cut. Her business would still continue but she wanted her horses out there. The timing was right as the twins were travelling around Europe. The horses would be moved without any trouble.

Lucia was now more settled and was thrilled that Liz had moved on and become stronger in herself. She adored her. Peter thought it was a marvellous idea and could see she was really settling. She and Lucia were so happy together yet still had their own space. At last she was at peace with herself.

He and Adam contemplated the last few months and the events that had taken place.

Rose had been forgiven as had Sam and he knew eventually they would meet again. It did not worry him as he knew Liz loved Lucia like she had never loved anyone in her life before. She was settled in the country she loved with the woman she loved.

Liz adored Lucia in a way she had never felt about anyone before. Sam and Max had had her heart but in the end they had broken it. She was stronger now than she had ever been mentally and felt she could take on anything. The marriage was over legally and she had settled into a wonderful relationship. They all still trained together with Michael and Sarah and now they all rode together. It was an exclusive expensive life they had and they thoroughly enjoyed it.

Nothing however could prepare her for when she would finally come face to face with Sam and later on Max.

Chapter 36

The book was a huge success as they had all predicated. Peter had ensured that Liz's best interests were looked after and had arranged a string of interviews to be held in London as long as Liz was willing to travel. She thought long and hard about it and eventually decided she would go to London as long as Lucia was going with her. Lucia now worked less and less in the hospital preferring to be with Liz as much as possible.

Rose was in London so she ensured Liz was looked after as Peter had another commitment. Liz did not mind as long as Lucia was with her. Rose had particularly ensured that Sam did not travel to London as she didn't want a scene. She was helping Peter out and could not let Liz down by parading Sam in front of her. She still had strong feelings for Liz and not for one minute did she want to hurt her anymore more than she had already done especially as it looked as though their friendship could survive.

Lucia never left her side. All the interviews were completed in the hotel. Radio and TV appearances were carried out over a period of a few days and Liz was relieved when they were finished. She was exhausted and just wanted to return home as soon as possible.

Susan was more than capable of organising the transport of the horses and in a matter of weeks they would be ensconced in their new surroundings. There was so much to look forward to for them all and

Michael and Sarah would look after the villa. Yes life was good and she and Lucia were in a place that she had never been in in a relationship before.

It was the final afternoon of interviews and they would be flying home straight after the last one. The bags were already packed and Liz waited patiently for the final reporter to finish up her notes. Lucia had settled the bill and met Rose on the way back to the lounge. Rose looked tired and was looking forward to being with Sam. She had missed her in the past week and could not wait to begin her own journey home. She just needed to say goodbye to Liz and she too would be off.

Nothing had been planned Sam had just travelled up to find Rose and take her to dinner. It was to be a surprise. She did not know that Liz would be there as she did not get too involved in the business side of things. Besides Rose had not mentioned Liz was there – on purpose. She had her own projects and did not feel the need to be involved in the business. She was a silent partner helping financially and certainly did not want to get anywhere near Max who was Rose's biggest contract. She knew Peter was looking after Liz but did not realise that Liz was at the same hotel as Rose. She hadn't made the connection.

Lucia and Rose walked into the lounge of the hotel chatting together where they could see Liz sitting in a very comfortable chair waiting for them. The reporter made her move and left happy with all her notes. She looked so tired and Lucia just wanted them to get home to their wonderful Italy.

Liz was oblivious to everything about her as she looked out of the tenth floor window at the view over London. They suddenly both stopped in their tracks. Sam had appeared from another end of the lounge. Lucia gently held Rose's arm as she felt her stiffen with worry and concern.

"No wait!" she said. Scared herself she loved Liz so much.

They looked on as they saw Sam stand for a while plucking up courage to go up to Liz. Eventually she walked up to her and looked at her with eyes that spoke volumes.

"Hello Liz," she said very very quietly.

Liz turned round to see Sam standing next to her she knew that voice so well.

Lucia and Rose were standing further back almost mesmerised as they both saw the look in the two women's eyes. It was a look of unfinished business as Liz looked up to her.

Eventually she spoke. "Hello Sam," in a very gentle voice.

They looked at each other silently for only a couple of seconds but it was long enough.

Sam almost had difficulty in trying to get any words out eventually she managed.

"Did you get my letter?"

"Yes," replied Liz, "I did."

"Can we talk about everything Liz? Please."

"Yes Sam. Yes you know we can talk, but another time now we about to leave for home we have a flight to catch."

Now Lucia and Rose approached them nervously. Rose immediately went to Sam who acknowledged her by taking her hand.

Liz seemed to know that Lucia was there and stood up to welcome her.

"Hi," she whispered in her ear, "let's go home," and kissed her oblivious to the other two. Lucia relaxed and held her kissing her back.

"We will talk one day Sam. Rose take care we'll call you soon." And then they were gone. Sam watched them as hand in hand they left the hotel.

Lucia had noticed the look on panic from Rose as the tenderness in Sam's eyes had spoken volumes of unfinished business. She loved Sam unreservedly but the look in Sam's eyes was enough to give her have a nagging feeling. The seed of doubt had once again been sown but this time in Rose's mind.

Rose above all realised that ahead of them all their paths were not quite as set in stone as they thought they might be.